W9-ADW-592

OBSESSION

OBSESSION

George Hayim

GROVE PRESS, INC.
NEW YORK

First published by W. H. Allen, London

Library of Congress Catalog Card
Number: 76-124397

First Printing

Manufactured in the United States
of America

OBSESSION

Chapter 1

I HAD BEEN SLEEPING NAKED FOR THE LAST TEN DAYS BECAUSE OF the heat. It was like the tropics. The days were hot, the nights were hot, and people complained. Heat to me means casual clothes, bare skin, fruit and ices, the beach. I love heat. I felt sorry for the maids as they sweated over the beds in the hotel where I lived. I had known them for years. They were tired and overworked and they smelled. I felt for them and knew what they were going through. In any other hotel I might have complained, but I liked them and understood. It's always different when you understand.

I don't work in an office; I don't work at all. I lay staring at the ceiling thinking idly: I've never wanted to work. I've wanted to be free to go anywhere and do what I want. But I wasn't able to. I hadn't quite enough money.

It's better now. I have a car, friends, lots of time, and I'm free. It's what I've always wanted. Now what did I want? The telephone rang. 'I'm working on a film—come and watch me.' It was Mirella. Good, something to do. I said I'd find her at the Café Colisée where it was taking place.

I slipped on an open shirt and strolled on to the Champs Elysées where I ordered a cold drink. I closed my eyes and sat bang in the sun. Paris was deserted. Just a few visitors. I started to doze off; I didn't know where I was anymore. Where did they talk French in the heat? Africa? Asia? Who were these others and what language were they speaking? Occasionally I opened my eyes. Everything seemed in slow motion, like the tropics.

People are dulled by the heat, that's why they keep getting run over. Many tourists were around, Germans, Swedes, white-faced, golden-haired creatures with black blodges for eyes—exotic birds, not women. Probably models. Swedes are models. Swedes kill themselves. Who has the highest suicide rate in the world? Why are there no male models? I tried to commit suicide once when I was young, but I don't want to die anymore.

Now that I've got all this time what shall I do with it? I could fall in love. I've never been in love . . . they say it's terrible—wonderful.

Who cares! I must get the meat before the butcher closes. But the butcher had already closed, I had forgotten 'les vacances'. As I walked to the next butcher I noticed the bakery was closed too. Housewives were complaining. I suppose it was a nuisance for them, trailing around until they found something open. I didn't mind—I rather enjoyed trying new places. Something could happen—a giggle or a row.

The shop that sold ice-cream was open. How good they were at midday when they came out of that whirling machine, soft and creamy, before becoming crystallised in the freezer.

I drove in my new car to the Bois. I left it outside Bagatelle and fell asleep near the rose garden. I slept a few hours and returned to the Champs Elysées. The sun seemed stronger than ever. As I made my way to where they were shooting the film, I saw a crowd. I pushed my way in to see what was going on. There was a large Rolls-Royce with a woman in it, dressed up in extravagant Edwardian clothes. It must be the star. Where was Mirella? I wanted her to know I had come. Maybe she could take a minute off for a cold drink. There she was clutching her camera—she looked brown and untidy. My friend Murray thought she looked like a monkey. She was sinewy, with tawny black hair. She might have been coloured—because she came from Kilimanjaro . . . sometimes it influences the way you look.

I called her 'elephant girl'. She looked as if she might smell of beast—I wondered how she appeared to others. I liked the yellow sack she had on—she was free inside it. By the time I got to the front she had disappeared. Everyone in the crowd was in open-necked shirts or sleeveless dresses. I rubbed skins with a dozen people. It was exciting to touch an arm with mine. I would look around—maybe they would too. Some did. I must be careful; no one wants a scene. But I love bodies. I've often bent down in a thick crowd, pretending to pick up something, to brush my lips against a hand. I must go slow. . . .

I was in the front now. The shooting had stopped but Mirella hadn't returned. On my right a young man leaned comfortably against a wall. He wore a cheap blue suit, the jacket over his arm. He was quite tall, not bad looking, a somewhat disagreeable expression on his mouth. I kept looking at him and wondered if he would look back. He might snap, 'Want my picture or something?' I could say 'Sorry, I thought you were André.' I knew what to do—I had been doing it for years. I went on staring. He had a heavy jaw, a straight nose with a hard curve to the nostrils. His hair sat on his head like a helmet. A gladiator. He must have seen me now as he looked towards me, the sun in his eyes. They were close together, hard, exciting and angry. A hunter? A panther, that's what! A panther! I laughed. It was jungle day. Mirella . . . Monkey Face . . . Elephant Girl . . . and now the Panther!

The mouth was full, sensuous and strong. We both stared in silence.

'You haven't seen a woman in a strange yellow sack, have you? Looks a bit like a wild African.'

He looked back mistrustingly. 'She was here.'

'Did you see where she went?'

'No.'

'Have you been here long? I mean are you part of the film? I mean, can you inform me? . . .' Then she appeared. 'There she is,' I said, putting my hand on his arm, to feel his muscle. He looked hard. I hoped he was. I dared not look to see if he had noticed the way I had touched . . . felt him.

I ran to join Mirella and we went to a café. The sun was setting and as we talked it caught her in the eyes, green and black like a cat's. I wondered how she and that boy would get on if they met in a jungle. Beasts in the night. They'd fuck!

Mirella told me about her work. Things were going well, she was a success. Good for her—what about me? Did I want to be a success?

I don't know, I don't think about those things much. We stopped talking and watched. Suddenly I saw my boy—I recognised the suit.

'I must dash!' I said. I sprang to my feet and ran after him. Just as he turned into the Métro I caught him. I put my hand back on his arm: 'Monsieur, forgive me—so rude of me—you were so helpful—I never said good-bye.' I was talking rubbish and he stood there, just looking at me. 'Now that I've found you, what about a drink?'

'I'm going to eat,' he said.

'Me too. I'm alone. Dine with me, we'll go to the market and get something "excitant".' I used the wrong French word on purpose because I wanted straight away to create some sort of equivocal atmosphere.

'Why not,' he said.

'We'll go by car.'

'Have you a car?'

'Any car you want,' I said laughing.

There were lots of parked cars there. I told him to choose the one he liked best. 'How about one of these?' I said coming to mine. 'I can open English cars easiest. Go on talking—I don't want to be conspicuous. I'm not a thief, don't worry. I just hate walking.' I fiddled around with my keys, making a great show, and finally opened the door of my Jaguar. He looked at me curiously and got in.

Most people don't have to find out about me, I tell all the first second. But this time I wouldn't. I'd keep him guessing. I pressed all the dashboard buttons and eventually got the car started. Here it goes, I thought. I'll take him home and get him drunk and make him talk. Then we'll do some wrestling around and it would develop. It usually does.

We stopped at the market and I gave him money to buy fruit and flowers. I'd get the meat. Cooking on a hot-plate in a hotel bedroom limits the choice. Steaks, cutlets, chops. I chose veal and wondered what he'd bring. He might bring nothing at all—he might disappear with the money. Maybe he's a liar, a hustler, who cares? Let him steal now, later he might take something more valuable.

He didn't disappear. He brought a few things and some yellow flowers.

'What's your name?' I asked.

'Edouard.'

'Mine is Jo. Terrible name, Edouard . . . only for noblemen and actors. Haven't you another?'

'No.'

We drove the rest of the way in silence. We got out of the car and entered the splendid hotel with its liveried footmen and marbled tables where I lived. He hardly looked around, it didn't impress him. Perhaps he was on his guard. But as I got to know him in the subsequent months, I learned he was impressed by nothing—not beauty, not wealth, not kindness. A good meal, perhaps, if *I* cooked it.

The hotel was a grand building off the Arc de Triomphe. I had lived there for years, all my family had. We had seen bell-boys become managers and managers die. The porters were my friends, often calling me by my Christian name and sometimes a nickname. They didn't respect me, but they liked me. I lived in a small attic room with a sloping ceiling. It was different from other rooms because it was mine, my untidiness, my friendliness, my rugs, my guitars.

We walked in, undid our packets, and I started to cook. Edouard told me his father was a government employee from Morocco. He himself had arrived in Paris with little money and had lived in a room belonging to his friend Michel. After a month he had found a job and moved into a cheap hotel.

I liked hearing him talk. He was gentle yet virile. He didn't smile much and he asked me nothing about myself. His eyes were cool and distant, yet he couldn't be cold with those hard, curved lips. He had a strong smell which I noticed now that we were sitting together in a small room. I liked it.

I ordered ice, put the cubes into an empty jar, got Edouard to squeeze a lemon and shake it all up. I frosted the rim of the glass by running the lemon skin over it and dipping it into the sugar. Edouard seemed interested. He found the drink excellent. I busied around with the food and occasionally, as I passed him, slipped my hand over his head. It was a good head, full behind and curving in at the nape of the strong but graceful neck. Although sinewy, he hadn't the physique of an athlete. His body was more subtle and reticent.

Again I moved behind him resting my hand on his head, this time a little longer. I stopped as I talked and worked my hand gradually down his neck under the collar of his shirt. There the skin was delicate and white, in contrast with the hardness of his brown face. He reacted. Dropping knife and fork on his plate with a clatter he said, looking straight at me, 'You're trying to make me, aren't you?' There was a pause.

'You don't have to put up with me,' I said.

'Every time someone is nice to me it's for that.'

'Who are *you* nice to, Edouard, and for what?'

We continued in silence. I cleared the table and prepared coffee. I had no idea how it would end, I just didn't know. But I was excited.

'A friend is coming to pick me up any moment,' I said.

'Then I'll go.'

'No. I want to talk to you.' This time I went to him, put my hand under his chin and tilted his head towards me.

'You're handsome.' He glared back, proud and insolent, and didn't answer.

After coffee I sat on the floor in front of the armchair where he was stretched out. I don't know what made me speak to him so boldly.

'I said I wanted to talk to you and I do.' I took his left hand and held it firmly, then I put it on my head which I rested on the seat of his chair. Something was happening—something important. This might be someone to have in my life, someone to care for, someone to look after, someone to love. Time, affection, freedom, money . . . what did I want? I wanted someone to *belong* to. Enough journeys, enough sensation. Now I wanted ties, roots.

'Edouard, are you listening? You're quite alone in Paris and you're young. I like you. I'm alone too, and I'm sick of it. Have you . . . the courage . . . the time, the authority . . . at your age, to receive me, to use me, to make me yours?'

All this time I was pressing on his hand so that it squeezed the tendon between my neck and my shoulder. It was painful and I was twisting my head and neck enjoying the pain his fingers were causing as they dug their way into me.

'Go on, man. Take me, own me, love me . . . no, don't love me. Let me love you, Take me . . .'

Then the blow came. He must have hit me with his right hand. I landed at the end of the room on the floor, my mouth full of blood. I could taste it. I covered my face with my hand. Edouard was standing over me. He grabbed a peach and hurled it against the wall where it exploded, bits sticking to the ceiling. I was shocked and trembling.

'That's done it,' I said, challenging. Something had clicked. I felt suddenly calm, vanquished. I believed in that second that I had at last found my place and a reason to live. I raised myself on my elbow and looked back at Edouard, then at the bits of fruit stuck on the ceiling and wall . . . then back to Edouard again. I had fallen in love.

As I stared tenderly at him the phone rang. It was Karl the American journalist I was expecting. We were to call on my friend Natalia and he would come over in half an hour. Edouard had collapsed into his chair. I was still shaking.

'Shouldn't we get tidy?' I asked.

He reached his hand over to my head, took me by the hair and drew me to him.

'Viens,' he said. With his free hand he slowly opened the zipper on his trousers.

Chapter 2

WE WERE STILL TOGETHER HALF AN HOUR LATER WHEN THE PHONE rang again. It was Karl, in the lobby. I told him to wait downstairs. Edouard washed, then I washed. We didn't talk. I put some eye-drops in his eyes to take away the redness. When we were ready I put my hands to his face.

'We're no longer alone. It's the first time I've ever felt like this. You have a responsibility now.' I laughed, he smiled. Then he did something that was to attach him to me in the future. He dropped his head like a stone onto my shoulder.

We joined Karl in the hall. After the introductions I made for the bar. Karl followed. Edouard said good-bye to him, then came to say good-bye to me.

'Are you mad?' I asked. 'Have I waited forty years for this, to hear you say good-bye? Get into the car at once! I don't even know your name. I'll never let you go, do you hear me? Never. You have a family now!'

We got in and drove to Natalia's.

The evening went smoothly. Edouard gave Natalia's daughter a bath. She looked so slight as she sat wrapped in a towel on his knee. Ten years of delicate girlhood in Edouard's arms. She's ten, he's twenty. In ten years *she* will be twenty. He might fall in love with her, he might even marry her. I'll be fifty. No matter. I'll have been ten years with Edouard. Then I can help them get married, buy them a house. I'll be on the inside. I don't want to be on the outside anymore.

I joined Karl on the terrace. 'What do you think of him?'

'Handsome,' he said thoughtfully, 'handsome.'

I was longing to tell someone about the last hour. The sock on the jaw, the peach. But it must be someone close to me.

When I had dropped Karl home, Edouard moved into the front seat next to me. I asked him where he lived and he told me, but asked me to drop him off before we got there. I made him spell out his name and address carefully.

'Do you need anything from me? Here's some money if you're short. But no hurry, we have time. I want to look after you. Everything is simple now . . .'

I was asked to Mirella's for lunch the next day. I asked him to come too. I said I would call for him at his hotel, but he said I should wait for him at the Châtelet instead. We agreed on the time and I left. I could not believe my happiness. Wait long enough, want badly enough, give enough . . .

I had hoped I would sleep late into the morning. It would mean that much less time to wait for our appointment. I could think of nothing else. A film would pass the time—but then I thought . . . better not. I remembered a story about lovers and a date they had He was so impatient, waiting was anguish. He went to a film, a thriller, and was so engrossed that he missed the date and never saw the girl again. He never got over it. It could happen to me now, but it wouldn't. I would arrive early, and he would arrive late. Yes, this time and the next, whenever we arranged to meet—I would wait, and worry that he might not come.

Maybe that was the way it had to be. I didn't mind. Let him tease me, keep me in suspense, let him do what he wanted. As long as he was there. I knew I was letting myself in for a lot of heartache, but there would be compensations. He would sleep with every girl in town, refuse to see me nine nights out of ten. But there would be the tenth. And even if there wasn't, I still didn't care. I would even work, he would have my car, take his girls out in it, do whatever he wished . . . But I would always be 'home' for him.

I rang up Murray, my best friend. He deflated me when I got too enthusiastic about something—a place, a woman, a tailor. He was always right; when I told him the story he was interested.

'Sophisticated thing for a young man from Morocco to do,' he said.

When I told another friend of mine he just said, 'What an act!'

For the tenth time I looked at my watch. I should go soon. It was Saturday. I dared not be late. I parked outside the Châtelet and waited. I had rung Mirella and told her I was bringing a new friend to lunch.

'Another of your brutes?' she teased. I was always bringing fellows I had picked up to re-wire, paint, or paper her rooms. After half an hour I decided Mirella would have no chance to form any opinion of Edouard because he hadn't shown up. I rang to tell her. 'Never mind,' she said, 'you'll find someone else tomorrow. I am in no hurry. Come late.'

I ran to his hotel, hoping he hadn't lied to me—I couldn't lose him now. Not now that I'd found him. The hotel was in a dirty street by the market. I was surprised when I went inside. It was both clean and quiet. I was happy he lived in a decent place, that is if he had told me the truth. An old woman sat at the desk on the first floor.

'Does Edouard Solda . . .'

'Fifth floor, room twenty-one,' she interrupted.

Twenty-one. He is twenty-one . . . life begins at twenty-one, then life begins again at forty-one. Go on, you fool, stop being an ass, it's just a coincidence. I walked slowly upstairs. I wanted to run, but I was shaking. My heart was beating wildly. It was absurd. I tiptoed to his door and opened it quietly, without knocking. He was fast asleep with his mouth open like a fish.

I should have been outraged by his bad manners. But right then I thought—nothing else matters. I went to the basin and dipped his face-cloth in the cold water. I sat next to him on the bed. 'Edouard, Edouard, Edouard,' I repeated. I wanted him to know it was a friend, not a stranger waking him. I wiped his face gently, starting with the eyes, then the mouth. I rinsed the cloth and returned, this time to clean the dryness from the corners of his mouth. Then I patted it. I liked washing him, attending to him. He grunted a bit and looked displeased. I peeled an orange I found on the mantelpiece. He started to speak, to ask who it was, and as he did so I worked a bit of orange into his mouth, the juice trickling down his jaw. He munched lazily. He looked as though he had passed out.

The thought even occurred that he might have been dead, shot through the head. NO, NO, not dead. Not even in fun.

I looked around the room. I wanted to know how he washed, how he slept. I wanted to remember it when I wasn't there. I went out on the balcony. It overlooked a corner of the market. The smell of peaches and melons filled the air. He might have lived underground, but he didn't. This is sacred, it's up high, clean, and next to heaven. I laughed to myself. The enchantment of love!

What else was in the room? A table, a chair, toilet things. A bottle of 'Pour un Homme' by Caron. I opened the cupboard. Here was the suit he wore, almost nothing else—he had nothing else. Oh yes—a tin box lying on the floor of the cupboard. He was still dazed. I shook him. 'Wake up! Tell me what's in that box?'

'Toute ma vie. My life, my pictures, my photos, my letters.'

I looked at the cheap thing. So this was his whole life. Does that make each thing there all the more valuable or less? What I didn't know was that I was going to spend hours and hours just touching it and holding it.

'Hurry up now. Get up and shave. We'll be late and I want you to look nice for lunch.'

'Je m'en fous. If I have to shave I won't go.' I didn't make an issue out of it, and in time we left.

Mirella greeted us without fuss; she was busy. Her hair was brushed straight back and she wore no make-up. She began complaining to me about the nurse who looked after her child. I just listened. In my mind I had already decided that she should find Edouard attractive. Of *course*, Mirella would. I went to the kitchen while Edouard took the baby outside in her pram.

'What do you think of him, Mirella?'

She looked at me quizzically. 'Nothing . . . nothing at all.'

'I'm mad about him! This is love.'

'Ass,' she said.

Later Edouard brought the baby back in his arms, she looked happy snuggled up in his big hands. When he put her down she started to cry. As soon as Mirella left the room I asked Edouard what he thought of her. He said he found her striking, but I think he realised she did not think highly of him. Maybe I was wrong.

Maybe he was of no interest to anyone unless one was in love with him. I was disappointed. I had looked into her eyes and then into his, and had invented a child from a love affair between them.

I must get hold of myself and stop dreaming. No matter. I had another appointment later on with some models. Would they like him better?

We got into the car. I sat in the back seat, Edouard behind the wheel. He drove off, but not before banging into the car behind and breaking something. It didn't upset him much. He didn't even apologise. It annoyed me, but I admired his calm *more* . . . or was it calm . . . I kept silent and we drove to the rendez-vous.

Amalia and Cornelia were everything one could expect from South America. 'Tropical Models,' I called them with their olive skin and light eyes. I had known nothing of them until the phone rang one morning and the porter told me to come down at once.

'Two dreams of beauty await you. If you're not interested let *me* take over.' A friend had given them my address, it seems. They came and they were here for photographic work. I liked them. The small one was bright and enthusiastic . . . the taller more elegant and charming. I was charming in return. I told them they sent out colour vibrations and they were amused. I wondered what these attractive girls would think of Edouard, of his cheap suit and unshaven face. But they liked him. Was he lovable or wasn't he? Maybe he was a conqueror after all. I saw him standing like a battle-scarred warrior, the models on their knees, clinging to him.

Now that Edouard had met Mirella and seen the girls, I had no reason to keep him longer. When he said he should be going soon, I nodded agreement. He said he would call. I said we would discuss our plans for tomorrow when he phoned. He *would* phone. Of course he would, at least to thank me or tell me what he thought of everything. He must. I waited three hours in the morning. He did not phone. Nor did he the next day or the day after that. I was distraught. I nagged the operators in my hotel, I left messages to say where I would be, and finally ended by not going out at all.

I was overcome by anxiety, then emptiness. Why this silence? I left messages in his hotel. I confirmed the messages.

Had the old woman forgotten to tell him? Had she been disturbed as she was going to write it down, and then forgotten about it? Should I go to his hotel and wait outside his front door? Suppose he wasn't sleeping there. He might have gone home for a holiday. This was dreadful. I'll write! Why hadn't I thought of it before? I mustn't sound too worried or hurt. It must sound quite ordinary, funny even. I started it fifty times; and still it wasn't right. Then the idea came. The child! I would write as if it were from Mirella's child! *That* would move him.

'You held me in your arms. You kissed me. I couldn't speak. When will I see you again?' I signed it with the baby's name. It was a stroke of genius. It had humour and pathos, it had love too. I then spent thirty-six hours of beautiful sunshine, lying in my room waiting for the telephone to ring. And then it rang. I could swear, the noise of the ringing was different. It was Edouard.

'Oh,' he said, 'getting at me through the child,' and he started to laugh. He hadn't been busy. He hadn't forgotten. He intended to ring back but hadn't got round to it. I thought it was wicked. He had time, he was twenty-one. There was so little time left for me.

I asked him to dinner. He said he would come the next night instead. We arranged to meet at eight-thirty.

'Don't be late. I'm cooking for you; and I won't wait.' What did that mean when I knew I'd wait ten years. 'And I'll run you a bath.'

'Chic, save me going to the public ones.'

The next evening I ordered ice at twenty past eight and tried to read. I couldn't. I kept looking at the clock. I tidied up. I looked at myself to see if I looked all right. Then I washed my hair, it always made me fresher and younger. I looked again, nine o'clock, none of it did any good. I was decomposing in front of the mirror. I would give him until quarter past nine and then go out. I was disconsolate. At a quarter past (people you love know exactly how to time the moment) he rang.

'C'est moi,' he said. I couldn't speak.

'I am with a girl in a restaurant. Come round with the car and drop her home.'

'Sure,' I snapped at him, 'I can come now, this second, and take her right to her home.'

'Chic,' he interrupted.

'Chic nothing!' I said. 'If you don't come this minute, then go fuck yourself.'

I'm not sure if he said 'Bon' or what. I'd just have to wait and see if he came. Whatever I did was bound to be wrong. He *did* appear, finally, walking nonchalantly into my room.

I put my arm around him. 'Glad you're here. Hurry with your bath.' (I wanted to say so much more.) I followed him into the bathroom as he stepped into the tub. I wouldn't leave him. He was lying in a mass of blue suds I had prepared.

'It's still a treat for me. We had no hot bath at home, then there was the army, and my hotel. So you see what it means.' I hoped he wouldn't wash too hard under his arms. I loved that mixture of his own smell and 'Pour un Homme'. It stayed with him as long as he stayed with me: till the day he left. Then, I don't know, it died, I died, the friendship died. But that was later.

As the water ran out of the bath he lay curled up with his face under the water like an embryo. He came to my room and flopped onto the bed, waiting to cool off until his whisky sour was ready. I couldn't keep away. I came to him and began caressing him. I ran my hands over his body and he twisted and turned. I ran my tongue down his legs to his feet, sticking it between his toes. He threshed around saying, 'Stop, stop, stop.' I continued till he shot up and whacked me across the side of my head. I thought he had broken my eardrum. It was a senseless thing to do. He didn't care. He didn't apologise, though months later he admitted 'That was bad.' Somewhere he must have a heart and a conscience, I thought. I still loved him. Time would show where he was vulnerable. Time? He might die before me. Had he been vaccinated against polio? I must look into it.

When I recovered we sat and ate. I put the food into his mouth myself. He chewed with his mouth open, as if to say—'I eat the way I want and I don't give a damn.' Later in London my friend Rachel said even that indifference was studied, like everything else about him. Then, I put my hand back to my ear—it was damaged. I didn't care.

Chapter 3

ONE DAY EVERYTHING SEEMED CHANGED. HE GAVE ME HIS OFFICE number, and we began meeting after work and having drinks on the Champs Elysées in the sun. It worried him having my car parked in front of the office, but he got used to it. Later he would sit in the driver's seat and drive off. Why not? That was his place, at the wheel. Yet only once did he ask me to lend him the car—to fetch his friend Michel for dinner. I now had a plan for him. He must have a home and we must start preparing for it, but it was difficult. He still kept me in doubt about our friendship, as he did about tomorrow's lunch or the cinema that night. Sometimes, after a happy evening, he came home with me, I thought to stay. It was next to his office and he saved a lot of time by staying. But at the last minute he would push past me and go. I'd follow him in the car, driving furiously along the Seine, past the Louvre and the Châtelet, till I got to the Boulevard Sebastopol, from where I would watch his room. The lights would go on, he'd brush his teeth, put out the light, and he would be asleep.

There was only one thing for me to do I was so tense, I had to let off steam elsewhere, find other adventures, but one's not free when one's in love.

The heat hadn't lessened and people walked about the streets half naked. One day sitting in a café near Edouard's hotel, I saw a Negro running towards me. He wore a torn shirt and his physique was spectacular. He laughed as he ran. I stopped him: 'I'll take you,' I said. A minute later we were in the car. He told me he worked in an African restaurant. I asked him home that night and he came. It started the same way—the whisky sour. I put on some records which I had brought back from Brazil, one, all drums and instruments with no melody. I had some of those instruments in the room, gongs, a pair of maraccas and a basket full of beans. One by one we tried them all, getting drunker and wilder. I turned the gramophone up. We got hotter and hotter, stripped off our shirts and started dancing and shaking. We fell on each other.

The telephone interrupted us. It was Edouard, Edouard who never phoned.

'Come,' he said, 'it is urgent.'

I asked him what had happened and he said he couldn't tell me.

'Money, police, what?' I asked.

'I'll tell you when I see you.'

We dressed, I had arranged to meet Edouard on the Boulevard Sebastopol. Before arriving I let the African off. Edouard was waiting at the Châtelet. Why? I don't know. He had said Sebastopol. Why was he here? It was always like that.

'Have a good time?' he asked, as the other left. I asked him to tell me what the trouble was. I didn't know what he had been up to, he might have to flee the country. I would help him, take him, I would do anything for him.

Slowly from his pocket he drew out an envelope which he handed me. It was addressed to a firm in England and contained a cheque. I felt sick. Surely he was not a crook. He was a decent boy. What then was this?

'I found it and I don't know what to do with it.'

I looked at the date. 'How long have you had it?'

'Three weeks. I meant to post it on and I forgot till today.'

'Why tell me? Why now and not tomorrow?' I asked, regretting the African interlude.

'Just to see if you'd come,' he was smiling.

'Give me the letter, I'll send it. I told you, you could count on me. Any time you need me, I'll drop everything and come. The day I don't it'll be over.' I preferred to have been fooled by him than to have ignored his call. I remember I was smiling when I fell asleep, thinking, He's got me, the bastard, but I am no longer alone. At least I have someone to watch—to live for.

I wondered how Edouard behaved with girls—did he have a place to take them?

'What about the one I was supposed to drop home that night, Edouard?'

'She has a room. I go there when I want to make love.'

'And when *she* wants to, Edouard?'

'I don't know. I haven't given her my address.'

'What kind of a relationship is that?'

'That's the kind. She can take it or leave it.'

What a caddish thing to say, I thought. Maybe I actually didn't like Edouard. I hadn't seen him do anything that could be called lovable since I'd known him. And in many ways he was mediocre. He had nothing interesting to say and showed no curiosity in learning anything new. He *was* commonplace, I thought . . . except to one who was mad about him. He still was young and handsome and . . . his complete indifference to me fascinated me. Once in a restaurant he had said to me . . . 'Stop charming the waitress . . . and the garagemen. Just stop being so charming. It bores me . . . you talk too much.' What was I to him? I spoke loudly. I was indiscreet and had a very strong personality. Did I *really* offend him. I was idle and neurotic. But I had something to offer. I spoke several languages, had connections everywhere and to Edouard I must have seemed rich. He was thrilled to be able to bathe at my hotel. And he had my car at his disposal. Perhaps that was why he continued to see me.

What did he want . . . or didn't he even think about wanting anything? He told me little and gave me little. At moments when I thought our relationship hopeless he would suddenly drop his head on my shoulder and I'd forget everything. Who cares who likes whom? Who gives a damn? He's here with me now, he's my friend. The rest? Who cares?

I wanted to help him, help his brother, his sister, his parents. This was no adventure for me. This was to be a whole new world.

I arranged for Murray Firth to see him. He would advise me. Edouard had been exposed to a lot of English of late and was bothering me about helping him to learn the language. I told him that was no problem.

'We'll find you a place to stay in England. You'll work, earn enough for your school, and stay a year as a student. Perhaps work in one of those peculiar owner-cook restaurants where everything is loaded with garlic and simmered overnight.' This amused Edouard. Now he wanted to go to England. I said I would discuss it with Murray.

Murray was due to bring Cornelia with him that night. He had taken her out earlier in the week and rather fallen for her. At one moment, as the restaurant where they were eating turned down the lights leaving the candles burning, Murray thought he had never seen anything as wonderful as Cornelia. He stared at her, wanting to touch her, to feel that transparent beauty. And she stared back—just past his ear.

'God,' he said, 'you're beautiful right now . . . so lovely. Your hair, your lips. I think you are the most beautiful creature I've ever seen.' She was looking at herself in the mirror, Murray noticed.

Then she looked at me and said, 'Oh, you should see me again. Sometimes I'm really beautiful.' Murray said he really couldn't face her that night.

In the end, there was just Murray, Edouard and myself for dinner. Edouard got on well with Murray. Murray is such a man and Edouard needed to respect people. He only respected people stronger than himself. I told Murray, in front of Edouard, that I wanted to do something useful for him and was willing to send him to England. Murray was against it.

'Languages don't help you get a job. They just help you to jabber. There are fifty million waiters who speak three or four languages. If you want to do something for Edouard, pay for a course at some night school.'

Edouard laughed. 'No, no,' he said, 'that's not for me at all.'

'Then why do you want to learn English?' Murray asked.

'Pour les filles—for the girls.' Edouard and Murray both laughed.

Later Murray told me not to interfere with Edouard and his future. 'He's a healthy, mischievous boy, he's amused by you and meeting a lot of strange new people. Leave things the way they are, or you'll be in trouble.'

Dinner was a success. I cook well and these were my friends.

Murray brought the wine. I don't drink wine, but a taste from the dusty bottle proved to me once again that Murray could do no wrong . . . where food was concerned. I told him so and he grinned. Edouard liked Murray and he opened up to him. In the middle of dinner Karl rang. He sounded in a bad way. He was temporarily out of work. Neurotic at the best of times, now he was worse than ever. He was almost in tears on the telephone.

'I don't know what to do,' he said. 'No, no, I'm not broke. I just sit at home and polish the floor.' I asked him over, but he refused, saying he couldn't face anyone.

Murray phoned Karl later, pretending he was not with me, and said he was coming round to dinner at my place. He said he wanted to see him about work. Would he come round? I asked Murray if this was true and he said, 'No, but I'll invent a job for him, anything that'll put him right.' So Karl came. What a strange, comic evening we spent, all eating together in my room. In the end Murray did an article, 'The Off-beat American Journalist in Paris.' He published it in the magazine he edited and through it Karl found work.

Over dinner Karl took a liking to Edouard. He insisted on showing him the night spots of Paris. I thought it might be fun for both of them. After dinner they left. Murray gave me a funny wink.

'Karl has fallen for Edouard,' he said.

'He's either mad or drunk all the time,' I replied.

'He is both, but I'm sorry for him. You know . . . poor boy from the wrong side of the tracks, bright and sensitive and angry and arrogant. Suicide attempts, analysis. Used as a stallion by that French woman when he first came to Paris, who could have got him so much work but didn't. She saw him after dark only, which was pretty bloody of her. Although at times I do agree with her, he is scandalous. One must be patient and understanding with neurotics . . . provided they don't ring up all the time. Anyway, he was a marine during the war. His father was dead, his mother had no money and was living on Karl's military pay. Some sergeant heard the story and offered to take him in hand. You should hear Karl imitating him. "Listen, kid—you're a handsome boy and you got no dough. Come with me on Saturday night and I'll take you to the bars on Eighth Avenue. You get picked up by the queer guys.

They take you home, want to fool around with you. You just say that it's O.K., that you like it, but it happens you need a loan of ten dollars. Then you come home with ten bucks and a full stomach. If it don't go so good wait till he goes down on you, hit him on the neck and take his gold watch. Or say you'll break the place up. You'll get your ten bucks, but don't get us marines a bad name." So he went with the marine and he was picked up. The man cooked Karl a fine dinner, talked to him about his mother and told him he had been to the village in the Mid-West where Karl was born. He got Karl to spend the night there. Next morning when Karl was leaving the man gave him his address and a dollar for the fare. And that's how it started.'

'Karl felt he couldn't accept the dollar,' Murray continued. 'The man had been so nice. Of course that was the end of his friendship with the sergeant, but Karl and the man still correspond.'

When he finished talking of Karl, Murray suggested we go to the Pergola Bar to see the Negresses. 'There's one with golden hair I'm mad about. She reminds me of my great love in Trinidad where I was a sailor during the war. I remember the night,' he said, 'it was carnival and we were all sloshed and she was in my arms and I was biting her ears and squeezing her tits and I said, "Say you love, go on, say you're nuts about me." She said, "But you don't even know my name, Baby." "O.K., what's your name?" "I'm Baby Face Nelson." Imagine how that went down, me in my naval uniform!' Murray laughed heartily.

The next day at lunchtime Karl telephoned. I hoped Edouard would ring me, but he didn't. It was better hearing from Karl than no one. He told me about his evening and he sounded happier. Murray had been right after all. I think Karl was falling for Edouard. Edouard came round the evening after for a while and said coolly, 'Karl is mad about me.' Karl then began coming round daily and told me all about himself. I couldn't tell him not to come. I thought he was pathetic . . . but interesting. I was a little afraid of him. But I liked him. He recalled the incident that started him on his course of psychoanalysis.

In New York, as a young man, he had a dream that made a big impression on him. He immediately telephoned one of the best psychiatric institutes and asked for an appointment. They answered that they regretted they were booked right up for the next six months and that they could only put his name down for a later date. Karl asked the price of an appointment and was told a figure that made an even deeper impression on him than his dream. Undaunted, he insisted on speaking to some doctor whose name he knew and even obliged the man to listen to his dream over the telephone. According to Karl, it was then the psychiatrist's turn to be impressed. Karl was immediately received and treated free. It may or may not have been entirely true, but Karl was convincing. I don't know whether analysis had helped him or not, but it had given him a marvellously effective vocabulary. Either one thought he was a genius or a bore. Edouard thought he was a genius. Murray thought he was a bore. I was a bit afraid of him. I found our friendship uneasy. He was sharp, precise and bellicose, and stronger-willed than Edouard. Yet once when I felt frustrated and vengeful by the way Edouard played around with me I stupidly threw him at Karl, in the hope that Karl would break him.

To my alarm Edouard did fall for Karl's dialectics. He found Karl a wonderful person. Karl crucified him. He contradicted him, accused him of being a narcissist, a whore, a ninny and a whole lot of other things. I watched all of it, knowing I alone had fostered the friendship. I had even arranged for Edouard to spend evenings with Karl, when I knew Karl would be half drunk and probably make Edouard drunk. I was playing around with someone I cared for, more than anyone I had ever met. I was mad. Worse, I was now excluded; forced to ask Karl news of Edouard. I had thrown Edouard into the wild, private, psychoanalytic drunken world of Karl . . . and I was alone. This had to stop.

A model we knew asked us all to a cocktail party. I asked if I could bring Edouard.

'Hope he likes girls, Jo,' she said. 'It's bad enough that most guys have no money, but when they don't go for girls either!'

Mirella was invited, Karl was invited, we all were invited. Karl refused. He spoke to me frankly on the telephone.

'This situation is becoming intolerable: I don't want us to become one happy family. I've got it bad—for Edouard, I can't stand it. I'm not coming. What's more, I don't know what *you* think your relationship is with him. He doesn't like being with you. He's told me so. He thinks you're weak and uninteresting.'

I felt crushed and betrayed. I pretended not to understand, and said light-heartedly, 'Oh, come to the party, Karl.' So! Edouard had gone as far as to discuss me unfavourably with Karl! I felt sick.

During the evening Edouard told me that Karl had got him to come to his home for dinner after the party. I had hoped to spend the time with him myself. It was my own fault. Had I not rung up Karl and said, 'Do what you like with that damn boy, teach him a lesson'? This was the result.

The model's apartment overlooked the Seine, there was a fine view of the Louvre from the left bank. It was a warm evening, the big windows were open and the atmosphere was easy. Paris was beautiful. I felt sick. I introduced Edouard to everyone. I did not want him to feel out of it. Mirella brought her baby because she didn't know what to do with her. Karl was in a highly nervous state. He said he could no longer stand the tension. He didn't know what I was playing at, or what Edouard was all about. He felt like taking the first plane back to America, he said and he left.

Edouard carried Mirella's baby into a small back bedroom, where a young girl was making up her face. I asked her name and introduced them. Her name was Jenny. She was English and rather pretty, but a common girl next to the sort of girls I had been introducing to Edouard. I have always liked English girls, they have heart and they are frank.

'Edouard,' I said, 'you want to learn English. Here's your chance!' They seemed to like each other and I left them alone. I returned once or twice to see how they were getting on. Neither of them seemed keen to join the rest of the party. Later I asked if both of them would like to come for a drive. I suggested all three of us go to the Place du Tertre in Montmartre. I said it would be fun. They accepted. I knew Karl expected Edouard later for dinner. I didn't want him to go . . . yet I didn't want him to leave Karl at home waiting for the telephone to ring. I had been through that too often myself, but I felt the time had come to show that I did not want Edouard to be with Karl when he could be with me. He was *already* largely under Karl's influence. He had often told me how fascinating Karl's conversation was.

It must have been ten o'clock when we were finally seated together in a café at the Place du Tertre. It was full of tourists . . .with the French students trying to pick them up.

'We're in the right place,' I said to the girl. 'You're a tourist and Edouard has picked you up,' I teased in French. 'Unless we show Edouard how charming we both are, he will be leaving us to join Karl's little psychotic world.' I turned to Edouard. 'You are supposed to dine with him, aren't you?'

Edouard said with some regret that he was.

'Well, you'd better go,' I advised, 'fascinating conversation is far more satisfying to you than our silly nonsense. I mean, *he* knows what you are *really* all about. Go and meet him . . . take the Métro. We can all go out some other time.'

The girl looked worried and sensed, too, that she was excluded from the conversation.

'Listen, Edouard,' I said, 'ring up Karl and put it off. Put the blame on some psychological trauma you're going through, but put him off. The man is a disaster to himself and everyone else. He's fascinated by his own words. Of course, he's twice as clever as I am, but do you really want to sit in a room and discuss what *he* thinks *you* ought to be, or do you want to enjoy an evening with us? But then,' I said, 'I don't know how much he has hypnotised you. Go and phone him, go and tell him something has happened. Tell him you cannot face him, you will ring him tomorrow, you must have time to think.'

And here I was, obsessed with him, yet wanting to get him off with this girl! Insane!

I took Edouard to the telephone and left him to dial the number. He looked a little ashamed of himself. Anyone who lets himself be talked out of a date is a shit! What about the person who talks him out of it?

I joined Jenny. If she was upset she didn't show it, so we talked. I liked the way she made no bones about finding Edouard attractive. She said she had had a few adventures in France and shared an apartment with two girl friends. She wanted Edouard and me to come round. She had a nice little body and she was real. Next to Cornelia she looked like a servant girl, but she wasn't next to Cornelia. Jenny was a human being; Cornelia was a thing, like so many professional models.

Edouard must have been gone twenty minutes. I was afraid Karl might yet win. I told Jenny I would go and find him, that he was obviously having a hard time over the telephone. I opened the door and spoke to him. He was sweating with the heat, the embarrassing conversation and the airless telephone booth.

'Come on, finish it,' I whispered. He signalled angrily that he was in the middle of a conversation. I took no notice.

I ran the back of my hand over my chin (a French gesture meaning 'La Barbe!'—a bore!) and then I wrote hurriedly on a piece of paper, 'All this so you can go and talk about yourself. Tell him you'll ring tomorrow.' He asked me to leave and I did. Ten minutes later he was back—he was staying with us. He had finally chosen. But by then it was too much for me. I asked him to drop me home and then to take Jenny.

'English girls are always taken home to the door. You accompany her,' I said. And I left. I was throwing her into his arms and I didn't care.

He came to me next day for lunch as if nothing had happened. It was a Saturday and he had no work to do. I didn't know where he had been. I was a little worried that he might have dropped Jenny home and then driven to Karl's in my car, but he hadn't. He looked very pleased with himself. Yes, he had had a good night and the girls were sweet. They had cooked for him.

'Bad food,' he said. But he had slept with Jenny. 'Do all English girls make love with their stockings on?' he asked.

I replied, 'Edouard, did you have a nice evening with the girls, were they friendly?'

'Yes,' he said, 'adorable!'

'Then why are you such a cad? You tell me Jenny slept with you, then you make fun of her because she didn't take her stockings off. You're a shit!'

The next day Edouard asked me if I would seriously see about getting him work in England. I asked him to consider his decision carefully.

'Murray is against it,' I said.

'What has Murray to do with it?' he asked.

'Nothing, except that when he says something, it's almost sure to be right.'

'I want to go. I'm sick of my job here.'

'Have you discussed it with your parents?'

'I'm twenty-one and I don't depend on them,' he said. 'I want to go to England.'

That morning we started phoning the British Embassy and the Consulate for information about schools. The best way was to enrol in a school, get a job at a bar, earn enough during the evening to be able to keep himself and take his lessons in the mornings. I told him I would pay for everything he needed and also get from my uncle a guarantee that he would have a home.

I bought some books in English and told him to begin learning the language.

'You already know "come on," "let's go," "fuck off," all you need to learn is how to join them together and you can speak English! Then you can go to London. I'll fix everything for you. When I return from Brazil you'll be speaking English.' I wasn't really convinced of his desire to go to England. I thought he was talking to keep me worried. 'What about your job?' I asked.

'I give them a month's notice, that's all!' he said.

During the month that followed he didn't confirm his intention of leaving, and I was in considerable doubt about his going through with it. Then it struck me as pointless, sending him off to England like that, all alone. What should I do in Paris and Brazil without him? Here was a chance for me to look after him. I started writing to restaurants and bars, but it was obviously more sensible to go to London with him. Of course! I would go, and from there carry on to Brazil, I was in no hurry, as long as I was in Brazil in time for Carnival.

Since I was now to accompany Edouard to London, I asked myself 'What am I going to Brazil for?' I was at an hysterical moment in my life when any destination seemed pointless. I just wanted something decisive to happen to me.

'What if I die on the way to London?' I asked him. 'You've given up your job and you're on your way to a new country where you know no one. What happens to you then?'

'I will be free of you,' he smiled.

That afternoon I put some money in a Post Office account I made him open. I felt I had interfered in the course of his life. I had to leave him with something to get along with. I'd like to think he was relieved but I don't think he cared either way. He didn't thank me. I told him he was like my son.

'Really?' he answered dryly.

A few days before we left Edouard arrived at the hotel with almost a hundred pounds on him.

'Take it,' he said. It was all he had. For the first time I knew he was coming with me. I took the money and left it in his name at my hotel. What if I died suddenly with his money in my name. I seek him out, he gives up his job, he gives me all his money, then I die and leave him jobless. Without savings. I must protect him.

I said, 'You must have a home—we'll get a home—I'll make a down payment. You can rent it and it'll pay itself. One day it'll be yours; you must start now. Where will you go when you fall in love? You won't have a home to go to. You know what it is in France. What I mean is, if you have no place to live together, you will probably lose a wife through it. Start now. Life starts today.'

I can't remember what I told him, I was so dotty and talkative. What I really wanted was to tie his life up with mine inextricably so that wife, love, mother, money, business, nothing could separate us.

'We will stay at my uncle's in London. He's an old shit, but he's pleasant. He'll try to swindle us, but we'll be comfortable.'

Had I been sure of Edouard's friendship, I would have taken an apartment for the two of us. I didn't need my uncle or anyone else. But our relationship was uncertain to say the least. I couldn't make plans for a long stay in London alone with Edouard. So I still wrote to my friends in Brazil to say I was coming, but I knew I wouldn't go.

Edouard wanted to take the car to London. He liked driving, but it was an absurd luxury for the few days I intended to stay so I booked a train and plane combination. He had never been in an aeroplane and the thought of it pleased me.

That evening Cornelia was in my bedroom when Edouard arrived. He went to have a bath and appeared in a thin dressing gown. Cornelia had washed her hair. She sometimes did that when she thought I was sick of her. I stood spellbound watching the shining mass of silky strands becoming drier and lighter in colour till they blew in a draught and I'd forget I was sick of her. She was sitting in the armchair that Edouard had sat in before he knocked me across the room. Edouard was arranging his hair in front of the mirror.

'He is rather divine, that frog, isn't he?' I asked Cornelia.

'Yes.'

'His body's good too,' I added. 'I know, I've seen it.'

'What are the legs like?' she asked. I had been talking to her in English in front of him.

'Edouard,' I said, 'Cornelia wants to know what your legs are like.' Insolently, looking straight at Cornelia, he pulled up his dressing gown and showed his thighs.

I could not persuade Edouard to spend the night with me. When he was about to leave I told him to go to Cornelia's room to say good-bye to her. I felt he could have made it with her. Every attractive man in Paris was after her. It was so like life that she, ambitious and calculating, should have refused them all and accepted Edouard. Later he told me he went to her room and stayed a few minutes.

'Why did you leave so soon,' I asked.

'She's not a proper woman,' he said simply.

The next day I went round saying good-bye to my friends. Mirella was disappointed.

'Why are you with that ass?' she asked.

'You may not like him, but your daughter does,' I told her.

'She's only pretending,' said Mirella. 'My daughter likes all men.' We kissed and I left her.

Murray wished me luck and said that I was better off in Paris than in London. Georgie Thompson brought a wind jacket to the station to give to Edouardo. Karl came too. There was a three-hour train journey to Le Touquet in a silver wagon and from there the plane over the Channel to England.

Edouard wore the wind jacket and a pair of tight corduory pants. His hair was tousled and untidy and the colours he wore didn't go with each other. One felt he wore them only for their warmth, with no eye to beauty. Karl was very moved by the departure; he stood at the gate being miserable. I didn't care. I had been hurt too. Now I was happy. Poor Karl. He'd get over it—I wouldn't.

The train started and I closed my eyes. I can't think why, but I was happy. I watched Edouard. He was imperturbable! Once or twice he gave me a wink of friendship—and that was enough for me.

Chapter 4

MY COUSIN ROBERT MET US AT VICTORIA STATION. HE DROVE US TO Uncle George's. We called him Blodge because he was a fat, round, squashy creature. He appeared to be good-tempered and surprisingly often was. What one forgot or foolishly overlooked was that just because he was genial, didn't mean he was a nice man. He made a price with us for bed and breakfast. It soon became obvious that I would be feeding everyone there. No matter! I liked Blodge's children, Robert and his girl friend Samantha.

Robert was there alone the night we arrived. Samantha came a little later and within an hour we were all sitting on top of each other in Edouard's room. Samantha took an immediate fancy to Edouard.

'What lovely lips he has,' she said out loud in front of him. Ten minutes later I went into the room and found her lying on her back. Edouard's head was over hers, his lips touching her mouth.

'He's so sexy,' she said blushing. 'Smells so strong, too.' I could have kissed her—she understood.

'What about Robert?' I asked.

'He's downstairs,' she replied. I thought that was very funny. I had meant what would Robert think of it all.

I made them supper, and they hung around watching us. Edouard lifted his eyes to heaven as he put the first mouthful down his throat.

'That's why I'm with you, vieux con,' he said affectionately. 'If only my father were here, and my brother,' he added.

'Yes,' I replied, 'if only they were!' He saw the joke and glared or pretended to. 'Don't put your father on a pedestal, dear boy,' I said in French. 'You'll also be a father one day. So let's drink to your father and wish he were here!'

'Never thought of that,' he said. Edouard then took a bath, everyone kissed everyone, and we went to bed. Though I was sentimental about his first night in London I didn't join him. I thought it was better not to.

I don't think Edouard had ever been in such a house before. He was brought up in a bungalow in Morocco and his room was in the Halles of Paris. But he slipped into new ways without effort. Finally we found the school, paid the fees and he started.

He was to take lessons until twelve, leaving him with the afternoons free. He was in no great hurry to find a job or to study English. He needed clothes and insisted on paying for them himself. He chose a blazer and two pairs of grey flannel pants. One was conventional, the other pair, hipsters, fitted him tight round his small, hard ass and I said I'd buy him those. He laughed and said I should buy him the ordinary ones. He'd buy his own sexy ones.

Edouard enjoyed his school—as I expected. He had more of the mischievous boy in him than anything else.

I took him over to friends who had a fine house with a Toulouse Lautrec and a Gauguin hanging on the wall. Edouard was not interested in either. Not even in the 'au pair' girl, a native of his own Morocco. They should have had something to talk to each other about. He kissed her in the cinema rather perfunctorily one day, but he never took her out again. London didn't interest him. He took the trouble to go to the Tower and that's about all. I finally stopped suggesting Windsor Castle or the British Museum. I made an appointment to walk down King's Road to find work for him. He was not enthusiastic. He made me feel I was dragging him from place to place and it annoyed me. Here I was, forty and independent, and I was the one rushing in and out of bars with a forced smile asking if there might be a place free. Edouard started complaining. I was tired but still not discouraged. I kept at it. I thought of my father and his influential friends in the Government, of millions changing hands at the ring of a telephone. I thought of my mother watching me wash some shirts in a bath years ago.

'To think,' she had said, wrapped up in a huge fur coat. 'To think

I sent my son to the best school in England only to become . . . And here she emitted a kind of sob, then carried on 'a dhobi boy!' I was at it again at forty . . . running around asking in little bars if they needed a waiter. Edouard wasn't helping. Goddamn it I bring him to England to get him a job so he doesn't have to live off me, and can keep his self-respect, yet I have to carry the bastard as well. Finally I got a tip from a woman who worked for a chain of restaurants called 'The Golden Egg.'

'Go to Earls Court at once,' she said, 'there's a vacancy.' It was dark by now, and I was cold and tired, but glad of the opportunity. Not so my French friend.

'I've had enough,' he said, 'I'm going home.'

'This is a job, Edouard,' I answered. 'You're living free—this is your chance to be independent. You don't need me if you have a job.' He wasn't listening—he had begun to walk away. I was furious, yet the idea of his being without a job and needing me pleased me. It was revolting that a boy I liked because of his manliness should have flunked in the face of three hours of job-hunting.

'Edouard, I'm sick of looking for *your* work. You can find something by yourself in the future. You are the one who doesn't want to depend on me. I don't mind it, I like it, but don't keep saying you want to be independent.' He didn't answer. He wasn't listening. I was being a bore and he wanted to go home.

The next day my uncle, who was always altering his house and garden, told me he was looking for someone to do some work on both. He would pay the same per hour as Edouard would have earned in a restaurant and the work was on the premises. I would be there. I could watch him, bring him cups of coffee, spoil him. He could work when he wanted. We wouldn't be speaking in English, but I would teach him what he wanted to know. I was a good teacher, even if he had said to me: 'Karl helps me. You don't.' Ah gratitude. 'Why don't you go back to Karl?' I had asked. 'I know why, you wouldn't be free.' Edouard looked at me from under his lids and smiled. This was his way of admitting he was being unpleasant. I just smiled back and the moment was over.

He started work the next morning at nine. My uncle had offered him a sum for removing some stones from his garden into the lane.

'Five pounds,' he'd said, thinking it would take him three days. But Edouard was strong and Uncle was furious to see the job done by the end of the day. Subsequently he paid him by the hour. After a week of lifting stones Edouard was unrecognisable. Already athletic, he became a mass of muscles. He looked less refined, squarer, maybe uglier. I liked him that way. I used to get him to stiffen his legs so his muscles stuck out and I could feel them. His shoulders swelled up and his neck got larger. He was like a mushroom that grew overnight and got bigger and bigger. I couldn't keep my hands off him. I barged into his room when he wanted to be alone. He'd throw me out. I would turn the whole thing into a joke by crawling back on my hands and knees like a dog barking. I thought it quite funny, but he didn't.

One day things changed. I was having coffee in a bar in Soho, called 'Le Bar des Voyous.' The owner was an Italian, so was the manager. There was a position vacant. I told them about Edouard and they asked me what he was like, the sporting type? The beat type? I didn't know what to answer so I took a look round the bar. Both the employees and the clients looked 'contemporary'—so I said I thought Edouard would be right.

'He's young and swinging . . . but honest and reliable,' I said. 'You'll be satisfied with his performance.' I felt like laughing hysterically at the idea of my talking about his performance! Wasn't that why I had changed my life?

When I returned to the house I described the bar and the job to Edouard. He showed no enthusiasm . . . but said he would go in the morning to see about it anyway. The next day he telephoned from the bar and said he had the job. His hours would be five to midnight every day. He wasn't too displeased I thought. Perhaps he liked the atmosphere . . . a typical student set-up. That night when he returned I cooked him a meal . . . his first day at work . . . and asked about the job. He just shrugged and wouldn't say much but I thought he might keep it. The problem was that the customers spoke French and Italian. Not much chance of learning English . . . but at least he was working.

In the days that followed I took him round to my friends. I introduced him to Ricki, a woman whose opinion mattered to me.

She had two young daughters, fourteen and fifteen and they spoke perfect French; I felt sure they would fall in love with Edouard. Ricki would surely appreciate him I thought . . . his walk, that sensual way he had of moving. But the girls didn't fall in love with him and when I asked Ricki what she thought she said, 'I don't like him—I don't like his face, he gives nothing of himself.'

Like Murray, Ricki seldom misjudged people. Murray's opinion was milder. He had said: 'He's just a natural mischievous boy. Understand and . . . leave him as such. Don't take him to London with you.' Neither could see *any* magic or mystery about him. And even for my sake they wouldn't consider him a friend.

'Les amis de mes amis sont mes amis.' No, 'Les amis de mes amis ne sont pas mes amis.' I worked it out. I went round and round in my head. One loves one's friends because of their friendship. My friends all respected each other. Sometimes they didn't get on, but none failed to register the quality of the other. To them Edouard had no quality . . . Why should my friends like him? He was something that had dropped into my life at a moment when I was vulnerable. Edouard was a need of mine. Edouard was nothing . . . just a body and a smell.

Chapter 5

WE HAD BEEN IN ENGLAND TWO WEEKS NOW. EDOUARD WAS GETTING on slowly with his English. He liked school and appeared happy. He was quite nice to me when we were together. I looked forward to his homecoming at night so we could spend a few short minutes alone while the others were asleep. Just to be able to cook for him and touch those hard legs or . . . even to see him. My trip to Brazil was still on my schedule but it was becoming more and more hazy and distant.

One morning I received a letter from Paris, forwarded by way of London . . . from some friends of mine, Ronnie and Rachel. They had written that they had bought a very comfortable and spacious house and invited me to come whenever I wished. I liked them very much. They were artists—futuristic I suppose one could say—remarkably educated but not stiff or formal at all. At dinner with an American philosopher they had used the phrase 'going out', meaning going into orbit, out of the world. That was a new expression for me. By the time I received the letter, they had arrived in London. I knew their new address so I rang them up immediately and asked them to lunch to tell me all their news. When they came they again asked me to stay with them . . . but I was happy where I was.

Looking around as he sat in the hall Ronnie said prophetically, 'No one could be happy for long in this house . . . mind you we are not as comfortable at our place yet but what we lack in carpeting we'll make up for in affection.' It was a strange thing for Ronnie to say. Some people always know what is going to happen. One puts it down to a sense of prophecy, but it is just intelligence and experience. Therefore it was almost a warning when he said, 'You won't be here long'.

Edouard happened to be home that day and he wandered in and out of the kitchen. I asked them what they thought of him. I remember saying, 'Isn't it extraordinary. This boy, brought up in Morocco with no sophistication. Look how he moves, it all comes naturally to him.'

Rachel burst out laughing. 'That boy doesn't do one single thing of which he isn't one hundred per cent aware. More . . . I would add that he doesn't move without deciding just how he's going to move. Anyway,' she repeated as she left, 'if you ever do wish to come and stay with us, you are welcome.' I didn't think I would accept her offer, but I was touched.

The following day I had a telegram from Natalia asking me to come to Paris immediately to be witness in a divorce case. Robert drove me to the station. I looked at the plane and for the first time I was afraid to fly. What if I died? Who would look after Edouard? I must take care of him. I had no capital, but I had saved a few hundred dollars and I owned a gold watch and a motor car. I must write out some kind of will. I couldn't leave Edouard with nothing. I wrote out a page saying that if anything happened to me, I wanted the car to be sold and the money given to Edouard, the watch to Robert and the rest to Murray. Then I got Robert and the maid (whom I adored) to sign it and I left.

It was wonderful leaving England—I always did feel a captive in the place. Now I felt free, free from England and free from Edouard. In England I was a servant. In Paris I was my old self again. I could be charming with the air hostess, pick up people and joke with them. I was unbridled, gay, relaxed. I wanted to lean out of the window and touch the sky. But it was just a few days. I had to go back.

Before leaving Paris I returned to my room to rest. I lay on the bed and looked round me. There were stains and things stuck to the wall. Only then did the scene come back to me. The day Edouard had punched me . . . and then thrown a peach at the wall in a rage—or in a feigned rage, how will I ever know? The bits had dried on the ceiling. I rubbed my jaw and I smiled.

When I got back Edouard greeted me with a lazy, 'Couldn't you have stayed away a little longer?' I had brought him back a few odds and ends from Paris—some 'Pour un Homme' and some underpants from Prisunic. I loved buying them because when the woman asked me what size hips, I was proud to say 'the narrowest.'

There had been few changes the short time I was away and the others at least had missed me, perhaps because there was no one to cook for them. I gathered the maid was now under Edouard's charm. Samantha, I'm sure, had spent a few moments locked up with him somewhere. And old Blodge had taken a definite liking to him. Things in the house could have been perfect, but I wondered how long they would last. Basically, Blodge was selfish and stingy. If I was willing to put up with him because of the comfort of his house, then I should never have allowed him to irritate me. But I did. Nevertheless, Blodge's affection for Edouard touched me.

Edouard had now fallen into a routine. He would be up and working in the garden by nine o'clock. Then he would bathe. I watched him, gave him drinks and rubbed him down. Then he took English lessons, ate somewhere in town and passed a couple of hours till he started to work at the Voyous at five. He would arrive home sometimes as late as one o'clock. That was the moment I longed for. Home! Fresh cooked food simmering especially for him. I liked to be with him after supper, but I didn't push it. He was tired, and the pleasure was only mine after all.

During the day when he was away I would stay in his room, tidy it up, go through his clothes . . . *and* his tin box. His twenty years were in that box—a picture of himself with his head shaven in the army, a photo of a girl he had been in love with, a letter from the firm he had worked for in Paris, service documents. There were one or two letters from his little sister, one from his father asking why he had chosen to leave the job he had taken in Paris, and then, at the end (and this I felt I shouldn't be looking at), some letters from Karl.

I didn't open them then and there, but in the days that followed I read those letters too. Karl wrote, 'I'm sorry Jo is driving you mad. Why don't you get a job and find a place of your own? If you are in any trouble, you know you can always rely on me.' I wasn't upset with Karl, but I was with Edouard. Edouard wasn't afraid of me; why tell *Karl*—why not tell *me* what he didn't like. I thought it disloyal of him, but maybe he was playing his own game with Karl. I justified my actions because I thought Karl had no business muscling in on my happiness in the first place. It is true that once I had said to Karl, 'Take him and break him, I can't.' I suppose it was dreadful to treat Edouard that way. Still, I wouldn't have interfered with Karl in love. Actually, what Karl had done was not so bad, it was the mere fact that he existed at all, that he was there for Edouard to write to and discuss me with. Fuck Karl.

I didn't tell Edouard I had read his letters. I was ashamed, but not too ashamed to stop doing so. Nor had I ever done such a thing to any other friends of mine. But Edouard was not a friend of mine; I was in love and people in love do anything. And somewhere subconsciously I knew that he didn't care for me, that he was with me 'for the ride' so to speak. But what ride? He never tried to get anything from me or ask for money or clothes.

I thought since he was good looking and manly, he might make some money modelling, or do some film work, but he wasn't keen. I had trouble getting him to register with the Police, at the Consul and all the other technicalities that are necessary when one is living in a foreign country. He had no realisation of the risk he ran by not doing so. He worried about nothing, as if he knew deep down inside that he would always get by. I asked him to open an account in the Post Office but he hadn't done that either. When in the end I got a friend to do a series of fashion photos of him he didn't bother to go and see the results.

At home things were developing. That sweet maid was about to fall in love with him too.

'He's a lovely boy,' she said. 'But he does smell strong. I don't like it.'

'Wait until you know him better,' I told her. 'You'll like it then.' What was I doing talking in that way. I was pushing her into bed with him. What else.

In order to be able to talk of Edouard publicly rather than keep my feelings to myself, I told everyone I was absolutely mad about him and that it was driving him crazy. I tried to turn it into a joke, a joke both to allow me to let off steam and to protect him. At the same time, I talked about his adventures with girls and said all I ever got from him was an occasional hug but more often a sock on the jaw or a slap on the ear. They believed the story.

Most people cannot resist boasting that they have succeeded in getting what they wanted. I wasn't really very interested in that. I wanted to be part of Edouard. Be in his life, see him, touch him, smell him. Sometimes when he hadn't time for me I would stick my hand down under his armpits and then smell my fingers. 'Vieux salud,' he would call me, and then smile with mischief, showing those beautiful, small, white teeth. It reminded me—I had to take him to the dentist!

One evening he came home by taxi. It was late and the underground had stopped. When he arrived he was very tired. I put him to bed. He pulled my head to him and gave me a friendly kiss. I went to sleep happily and was awoken by Uncle who was wandering about the house complaining.

'Get the frog up. He must remove the stones in time. The truck is coming tomorrow at midday.'

'I'm afraid I can't, Blodge,' I said, irritable at having been awoken so brusquely. 'He came home late last night. But he has neither school nor work tomorrow—he can do it all then.'

'No, no, no,' he answered, 'he must do it now.'

'Well he isn't going to do it now, and you're not going to awaken him,' I said annoyed. 'Other things matter in this world besides your stones. Leave him alone.'

One thing led to another, and I blew up. 'It's obvious why you have no friends. Your wife and family find you intolerable, you would be hard put to find anyone to go to your funeral, which will be any moment if my curse works.'

'If you feel like that, you'd better leave,' he said.

'That has already been decided,' I said, and furious I started to pack my things. I was terribly upset about the row because I was comfortable here and so was Edouard. Also, I didn't know where to go.

I rang Ronnie and asked him if his offer still held. He was delighted I had quarrelled with Blodge.

'Come at once,' he said. Edouard woke and I told him I was leaving. Uncle interrupted with, 'Oh, HE doesn't have to go.'

I repeated, 'Edouard, Uncle says you don't have to go,' and before I could continue he said, 'All right, I'll stay.' I was shocked. He was there through me. I had done everything for him, and now I had had a row with that fat ass of an uncle of mine as a result of protecting him. Instead of saying, 'I shall leave too,' he was saying, 'I'll stay.' What kind of friend was this? I only saw him in the evenings and the mornings anyway. When would I see him now? If only I could take him to Ronnie's. If only he had said he wanted to stay with me, then I would have something to work for. I left the house that morning—Edouard went to work and I went to Ronnie's. I was miserable.

Chapter 6

I ARRIVED LADEN WITH PRESENTS; FRUIT, A JOINT OF MEAT, A gramophone record and all my luggage.

'Where is your friend?' asked Ronnie as I walked into the house. 'We were expecting him. Oh well, he can come any time. Come in and we'll talk . . . I have so much to do, as you'll see . . . in fact, you can see already,' he said pointing to the entrance of his house. It was one of a row of big, sad houses overlooking a garden square. It was November and not a leaf was on a tree. The district was one of the dimmer ones of London. In previous years, it was known as a 'bad' district; knives and foreigners! One part of it was reserved for Irish labourers, whose drunken adventures were too many and too tragic to recount. The other part was Greek and Cypriot. One was surprised to enter a Greek barber's and hear Greek music and see Greek writing on the window of the newspaper shop. Next door there was a Greek butcher and a Greek general store, where they sold wines, olive oil and baklava. It was strange but fun for me to speak the language and a joy seeing fresh salads from Cyprus in winter.

Although it was still a poor district full of houses that let rooms, times were changing. London was already being cleaned up. And some brave pioneers such as Ronnie and Rachel had the good sense to invest in a house here. The prices were low and the houses were strong nineteenth century buildings of four or five storeys. If one missed the last underground the distance from the heart of theatreland was barely two miles. For Edouard returning at night, it would be perfect. Three stops on the underground and he was there, as opposed to the seven odd miles to Uncle Blodge's.

For me, there was no question of him staying on at Blodge's. He had to join me. That's why I had come to London. If he didn't care whether he was with me or not, I'd have to arrange things so that he would want to. I'd make it more convenient to be with me. In the meantime, I would look around, see to his room, and prepare it.

Ronnie's house was in the early stages of being put in order. The entrance door on the road was the most battered, discoloured one on the street, and they were all in bad shape. The flap of the letter-box was missing, so there was a draught from the road. I noticed the floorboards were covered with dirt and I thought that was a bad sign. I had often seen Ronnie in different parts of Europe—I knew him as erudite, frank, obsessively clean, energetic and funny. This mess didn't seem in keeping with the personality I had attributed to him.

Was Rachel responsible? I had never really understood her. Her clothes were strange, her walk was curious, her age uncertain. I knew she was clever and made dry remarks. Weeks later during a conversation with me she said, 'You know, dear, in Paris years ago, when I had serious personal problems, you were the one I telephoned. But alas, you were not there.'

'Why me?' I asked. 'You hardly knew me.'

'I knew you alright. *You* didn't know *me*, that's all.' It touched me, but I had no special feeling for her at the time. She was strange with avant garde plastic coats and leather skirts and summer dresses she wore in the middle of winter. Her green nails, her surprising hair styles, her dislike of long-lasting clothes, and her passion for modern form. I thought of her as a Bohemian and I accepted her because she was with Ronnie.

Ronnie was of average height, his body like a Florentine statue. Rachel looked as if, found naked, she would be like a Renoir. But later, living in the house together, when I saw her through the unfinished ceiling of the bathroom, I realised she was very tiny. I hadn't noticed her breasts—at the time I wasn't particularly interested. But in my subsequent bad moments Rachel used to come and sit on my bed and give me a tranquilliser to calm me and explain why things were going wrong. I would put my arms round her and put my head on her breasts, and it wasn't till then that I noticed how marvellous they were.

We did a tour of the house. I was relieved to see that the terrible state of dust below was not due to Rachel's slovenliness, as I had feared, but to the fact they were pulling their home to pieces and rebuilding it. For the moment the only room that was almost finished was the sitting-room-kitchen. It was a vast room painted white and lit by steel studio lamps. In front of each window was a step made of a long pipe coiled like a radiator lying flat on its side. There were no curtains anywhere.

'I hate curtains and furnishings,' said Ronnie. 'Just calico blinds, that's all.'

'Pictures?' I ventured.

'Certainly not!'

'What about the white walls—how long will they stay white in London?'

'When they're dirty we'll wash them; when they go yellow, we'll paint them again.'

I was fascinated—this was new to me. But after all, they were young, creative and modern. There was little they did not know about shapes and forms, consistencies and colour harmony. I was out of their orbit, but was delighted to be near it.

The kitchen was not ready. There was a steel trolley for the kitchen utensils and an old gas stove—so odd next to the modern shell of what was to be. The kitchen was part of the sitting-room. It had the same parquet floors, and by the time Rachel had finished explaining how the kitchen would look when ready, I thought I was living in a space ship with sheets of steel and lights coming out of huge heavy glass frames fitted into the wall. Pipes ran through the middle of the ceiling in the kitchen up to the bathroom above, and continued into the second bedroom above it. The plaster had not yet come and newspapers were stuffed temporarily into the gaping spaces round the pipes.

My own room was large and bare. They had not begun to fix it up. There were no cupboards and it was impossible to sweep the floor as it was rough and splintered. Rachel must have read my thoughts.

'It is uncomfortable, but it is your home. No one can ask you to leave, and the bathroom works. This room is yours—you can do with it as you wish, bring home whom you will. I ask you but one thing—don't bring women. I don't like women for women's sake. And,' she said, beckoning me with an authority I didn't expect from her little frame, 'I want to see no chocolate, no cakes and no fattening foods. Now I will show you Edouard's room.' She took me to the basement, to a nice clean room. Then they both went out and left me to myself.

Edouard had my telephone number and I hoped he would ring me, but he didn't and all evening I boiled with anger at the thought of us being separated. Rachel insisted I take a sleeping pill, so I did. I could ring Edouard in the morning—what was one lost morning in ten thousand that were going to follow?

The next morning I waited until Blodge was supposed to have left the house and I rang. Blodge answered. I was short on the telephone.

'Give me Edouard,' I said.

'Wait a minute!'

'Give me Edouard, please,' I repeated.

'Oh, er,' he stuttered, embarrassed. 'I'm afraid it's difficult.'

'Just put him on the line now,' I said angrily.

'You don't understand,' he said. I hung up. How dare this shit interfere with me and Edouard? I'd kill him. I'd denounce him. There were enough things I knew about him to make him cringe with fear of discovery. I waited raging and at a quarter to eleven I finally got Edouard on the telephone. He was in a jolly mood. I asked him to come to lunch and he said he would after school.

I watched the road from the window till he arrived. It was a sunny November day. I saw him coming from the distance. His hair seemed longer than when I had seen him the previous day. He walked with ease and nonchalance, a feline gait. How could Mirella have seen no charm in him? Robert's girl had, the maid had, that girl from Morocco had. Yet Mirella was a magnificent creature. Just because she and Natalia saw nothing attractive in him, it did not mean anything. What about all those other girls—in fact, everyone he had met in England so far had found him attractive. Yet who were they? Were they anything at all compared with the quality of these other two women? Then there was Peggy Ainsley, an ex-model, still a beauty and mad about young boys. One day when she was returning from America to Paris I took Edouard to meet her at Orly. He found her terrific. Later when I asked her about Edouard she shrugged her shoulders and said, 'Young French boy—cold and indifferent. Forget it.'

I watched until he turned into the house and I couldn't see him any longer. 'Be kind to me,' I prayed. 'I want so little from you, so little.' Ricki Madison had said the contrary. 'You want too much from him.' 'But I let him do what he likes, sleep with whom he likes, go where he likes.' 'I let him, I let him,' she minced. 'That's already a mistake. Furthermore, whatever you want from him is too much. You only have a right to what he wants to give you. You cannot make rules. You get what you are given. If it isn't enough, suffer or give up.'

And here he came now, this tall, athletic, slovenly, hirsute young man, walking down the street towards me, and who was I, an unbalanced, idle, obsessed man, to decide his life and future? Everything seemed to be so loaded against me. 'I will do everything and anything to have this boy near me, anything.' What was I talking about? I was hysterical, sick, mad. He rang the bell. I wanted to jump the fifty steps and land on top of him. I forced myself to go down slowly and open the door quietly.

'What fun I've had,' he said. 'What a horrible old miser that uncle of yours is! I have such a story to tell you.' I took him by the arm and hugged him.

'Tell me, tell me everything while we eat; and leave that place as soon as possible. There's a room for you here.' He took no notice and went on with his story.

'Last night I brought a German girl home. Your uncle came to my room at eight o'clock in the morning with breakfast. Yes, he brings me my breakfast. Anyway, he probably wanted me to get up and work in the garden. So he came in and brought the tray. Then he looked at the bed, saw the thin arms of that idiotic German girl around me and didn't know what to do. He fumbled and spilt the coffee and walked out and in again and then finally left the coffee and walked out of the door. An hour later, just before you telephoned, he called me. By that time Gisela had left and I was alone.

"Now Edouard," he said, "I'm afraid I can't have this going on in the house." So I said I would leave.

"Oh, no, don't leave . . . but after all, I can't have you using the room as if it were a double room. You took a single room here."

Edouard burst out laughing. 'You see, it wasn't the fact that I'd brought a girl home at all—it was just the idea of two of us sleeping there for the price of one. I told him I would leave anyway, as it was rather expensive for me, but he reduced the price, so I said I'd stay.'

'Why should you pay that money when you can stay here for nothing? It's not carpeted, but you have a room of your own and your food. It makes a difference of at least seven pounds a week to you. You could start buying a home with that money. And I want to be with you, that's why I came here.'

I don't think my arguments touched him in any way. It gave him no pleasure either to be with me, or to save the money, though he saw objectively that it would be a saving. He seemed, in fact, delighted to have a room of his own at Uncle Blodge's; all the more I felt since I wasn't there. But I begged him to join me as quickly as possible.

'I shall be leaving for Brazil soon enough, I only came here for you. Also, my uncle will throw you out the minute he has someone better. Dammit who is your friend? That shit or I?'

'Oh well,' he said, 'I'll come—sometime.' I asked him to come at the end of the week since he had paid his rent. He didn't answer.

In the next few days I saw him only occasionally. I almost went insane, so I went to the bar where he worked. He received me with embarrassment.

'I don't like you coming here,' he said under his breath. 'I wish you'd go.'

'Put up with it,' I said suddenly furious. 'You'd better come tomorrow, we'll discuss it and a few other things as well,' I added significantly, although I didn't know what to discuss 'as well'. So he was alright, he didn't want anyone around, he was free. But I had found him a home and done everything for him. How dare he now enjoy my uncle's house and work at the bar, when he never had the energy to go and look for a job. Why should he be content and me miserable in a town I loathed.

One of the other lads who served in the bar came in interrupting our conversation. 'Ah, Lucien,' shouted Edouard. 'They are superb, your boots—Oh là là c'est quelque chose! They're really something.' Lucien was the other barman, more lively than Edouard but not as handsome. Between the two of them they were a choice for any girl looking for adventure. They loved comparing clothes and shoes, as kids do. Today was Lucien's day. He came in wearing a pair of pigskin brown boots lined with white wool that protruded over the edge.

'How I'd love those,' said Edouard, and then went back to his work.

Of course, I went straight to a shop that sold surplus stuff and bought a fine pair of lined black boots, the type Nazi officers wear in films . . . the sexy kind. Great, big, black boots lined with sheep's fur. I got terribly excited putting them on and more so at the idea of Edouard putting them on. I would put them on him myself. We'd have a mad afternoon when he came tomorrow. How silly to argue about anything. He'd soon be back and I'd be alright again. All would be well—I shouldn't worry.

He came the next day at two-thirty. He was wearing a pair of corduroys, a sweater I had given him, and a wind jacket. I closed my eyes with relief when I saw him coming. Everything was prepared. The whisky sour, the bubbling hot soup, the huge veal chop, and from the Greek shop some Rocco salad Edouard had never tried. But he would—he would come to Greece with me that year and the next year, he would come . . . and then the ring at the door. I ran down, opened it, and threw myself into his arms.

'You wonderful, beautiful, shitty French frog, I love you today. I really do.' He was amused and I took him up to the sitting-room to the sofa, brought him his drink and put on a record and told him I was preparing the room downstairs. He was not to throw all his money away, and if he did, I preferred he threw it into the gutter rather than into the pocket of my uncle.

When he had finished his second whisky sour—and they were both very strong—I asked him to take his shoes off and close his eyes. I went outside, fetched the boots, and with his eyes still closed I slipped them onto his feet. He was delighted. I made him drink wine at lunch and after the meal I spent an hour with him. He promised to come at the end of the week to stay.

And then it happened—for the first time since I had known him. I cannot put it down to drunkenness. No, he was not drunk, he knew what he was doing. It was I who didn't know what he was doing. I cannot forget it. He was standing close to me, a little taller than I. His eyes were not two inches away and he was staring hard and smiling—smiling that diabolical smile of his with his eyes flitting rapidly over my face. He suddenly took my head, held it in his arms and kissed me—fully, deeply, with his eyes closed. I always close mine, but this was a complete shock. My eyes were open. What a thing to do! What a thing for him to do. Why had he done it? It was a joke, but it was a terrible joke. He must have done it the same way he had knelt down in front of Karl.

I didn't know what to say after that. What would happen next? It was like that book of Montherlant's, where a woman calls on an author she doesn't know. He lifts her and rapes her on his desk. He never gives it a second thought. But she, poor tragic thing, goes crazy. She waits for him and she comes and she writes love letters and insulting letters. She hankers and longs and aches and prays and she never, never sees him again. She thinks of nothing else and he never thinks of her. Edouard had kissed me once, suddenly and for no reason, unless to have the fun of watching my reaction. Edouard, who only liked women, had kissed me. I wished I had never read Montherlant's book. What was going to happen to me?

Chapter 7

IT WAS, IN FACT, TEN DAYS BEFORE HE CAME TO STAY. I THINK WHAT finally made him come was the pure repetitive act of giving my uncle money for the rent and realising that at the end of the week he had earned ten pounds . . . and spent them. I had one very vicious and exciting scene with him before he came. He wore his black boots daily, but he never cleaned them. One day after lunch he was full of drink and good food and he became playful.

'Clean my shoes,' he ordered peremptorily.

'Clean them yourself,' I said. He grabbed me with both hands and glared at me with his green eyes looking wild and bloodshot.

'That's your job,' he said. 'It's your job to do everything for me.'

'Fuck off!' I said. He took hold of my right hand and twisted the fingers backwards. The pain began at the fingers, went to the wrist and then when he had screwed my arm right up behind me—I groaned as I felt him pressed against my back. It was, for me, the pain, the warmth, the nearness, the hurt of love. I gave in.

Giving in to Edouard was no dishonour at all—it was, in fact, all I ever wanted to do. Of course, it lacked pride and dignity, and of course, I was handling him the wrong way, but this was where my pleasure lay. What was the point of enjoying a success, a victory, a relationship where I was respected and feared, when really I only felt pleased if he took me for granted. I would have liked a middle course, but that was not possible. Edouard, who had no intellect at all, but all the cunning, all the primitive sense and intuition of an Arab (which I accused him of being when I was angry), knew exactly how to treat me. He never gave enough of himself and he never showed his true feelings for me.

Right now he was playing games, and I love games so I played. Unfortunately when he played games he played with complete disregard for my limbs. A wild swipe and I'd go deaf for a week, a bang in the ribs and I'd double up. Now here he was, on top of me; he punched me, his eyes demented, and I think he was smiling. Yet I would give up everything to keep this boy in my life.

The great day finally arrived, the day he was to come. He had stayed away at least five days longer than necessary, and I had hardly seen him. Of course he worked late, of course he went to school, and of course he wanted to feel free. But I felt he could at least have given me the pleasure of seeing him once a day. I had teased him at various times saying, 'After all, Edouard, a boy used to the best of things in life is hardly going to put up with living in a basement with people he doesn't like when he is earning enough money to keep himself in a carpeted suite in a big house in a swanky district of London. I mean, how can a young man live anywhere but in a nice bourgeois wall-to-wall carpeted apartment?' He took the teasing well. It was easy for him to take anything to do with me well, since he was indifferent to me. I should have been more severe with him from the start and I should never have passed over his disloyal behaviour at Blodge's. I should have said, 'Pack your bags,' and that was all.

I thought of this as I unpacked his things. Edouard hadn't the education to value certain codes of behaviour, or else his moral code was so elastic that it could always make excuses for its failings. I needed time. If you care for people and if you're patient with them, you will educate them to better things. I did not then realise at the time that what you do for someone you are in love with does not have the same value as what you do disinterestedly. The moment love plays any role in a situation, everything is turned upside-down. There are no more rules—people behave abnormally. Sweet people become vicious swine. I felt this happening to me. I knew I was doing the wrong thing, but I hoped and thought and really believed things would be the way I wanted them to be. I had once told him, 'It's all for you.' He had answered, 'You plan and you plot and I'm the victim of your obsession. This is no friendship; you only want things to go well for me through you. You want to be a part of all I do.' It was true. He was not French for nothing. He saw clearly and he said what he thought.

For the moment, he hadn't a bank account and he hadn't a permanent address. I had to look after him. Then I would leave.

Edouard adapted himself as easily to the new house as he had to the old one. Sometimes he was pleasant and sometimes not. He told me little of what he was up to and he hated me going to the bar. I had again asked him to register and he hadn't. As the days passed I was displeased that he had made no effort to help in the house. He never offered to carry anything or fetch food. I complained to Rachel.

She replied, 'We don't need anything from him—leave him alone.' Nevertheless, I thought he should spare a thought for someone else. How could he stay with people he didn't know and never offer to help?

I used this point once or twice to start an argument with him, and on one occasion he became icy and within half an hour he had packed up his things and was leaving the house. He had, in fact, telephoned my uncle to say he was returning.

'I'm sick of you,' he told me. 'I want to be on my own and not be nagged and badgered and asked to pass by your room and say goodnight before I go to bed. I don't want to have to do anything. I want to stand on my own feet.' I was shaking.

'Is this the way to behave?' I asked him softly. 'You refuse to pull your weight and you threaten to leave like some petulant tart. You say you want to stand on your own feet, but you go running to my uncle, who made me leave because of you. Now you're going back to his house standing on your own feet! Coward! Go out and find yourself a room, if you must, but don't go back to my family who took my money to house you. You want to be a man! You're a traitor and I despise you. The agony is that I love you and I don't want you to go.' The thought of him leaving and my breaking with him, made me feel sick. I could hardly speak. My voice was shaking and I could no longer see straight. I remember getting up and going towards him on the landing.

'Telephone, Edouard, that you're not going. I'll go to pieces if you leave.' He seemed affected by my speech and he telephoned. I went to my room and collapsed on the bed.

That night he came back from the bar full of enthusiasm and made no reference to the scene that had taken place that morning.

'I've found a girl,' he said, 'and I think she likes me.'

'Oh, Edouard,' I reproached, 'it's always "I think she likes me." Why isn't it "I like her and I want her." I hate this attitude where the man waits for the woman to make a pass, then turns around and says, "I think she likes me". So unmanly.'

'Maybe,' he said. 'But I think I'm a bit in love with her, too.'

'What's she like?' I asked.

'Pretty. Half Austrian, half Norwegian. I'm bringing her back tomorrow night.'

'OK. I'll fix you up some dinner.'

'Do that,' he said.

They came in at about one in the morning. I had hoped she wouldn't come—I would have that much more time with him—but when she did, I didn't mind and I rather liked her. She was shy, well brought up and pretty. I was irritated by Edouard's behaviour with her, adolescent and attentive, on a boy and girl romance level. Silly, juvenile rubbish! It was false, Edouard was false. Oh, maybe everyone is false when trying to go to bed with someone. I might be sick watching *myself* trying to operate, for that's what it was all about. He was a little nervous in front of me, but I behaved alright. I left them and went to my room after dinner.

Shortly afterwards Edouard joined me. He had taken her down to the basement room and told her to wait for him there. He sat on my bed and asked me what I thought of her.

'Quite pretty,' I said. 'Don't ask me what I think of you, you big fraud.' 'Comedian' was the word I used in French. It was a better word. He was in a good temper and gave me a friendly hug.

'I want to borrow the hand cream,' he said.

'Have you gone mad, Edouard? What on earth do you want hand cream for? I'm the one who does the washing up.' Edouard looked smugly at me.

'I want no roughness on my hands when I caress her. I want to run them softly over her body, her stomach, her breasts. I want it to be gentle, slow, delicate. I like a lot of preparation, you know.

I don't want to just fuck.' As he spoke, I thought he looked more and more unpleasant. Firstly, I thought it was caddish to talk to me of what he was going to do to her; secondly, he might have been saying it just to annoy me or upset me. It didn't upset me. I hate caddishness and it angered me.

When I had left Blodge's and he was still there, he had told me how that sweet maid had prepared his food and his clothes, and how she was in love with him. I told him not to tell me such things. I didn't like it—he should be more of a man and less of a vain ass. And here he was, sitting on my bed, rubbing and twisting his strong hands with their sensuous fingers describing how he was going to caress the girl.

'Fuck off, Edouard,' I said. 'Don't leave that girl alone in the basement of a house she has never been in. I hope you have a foul evening.' I slept like a log. If he could talk like that, I had nothing to worry about and besides, he was living here with me in the house.

The next morning at eleven Edouard wandered into my room to ask me for some things for the girl—some Kleenex and some cream —and with that, they locked themselves up in the bathroom. I would see how they behaved after having spent the night together. I crept slowly up to Rachel's bathroom and crawled gingerly across the floor.

Where the pipes passed through the ceiling, the space around them had not been plastered over, balls of newspaper filled up the spaces. When I realised this I had said to Rachel, 'You can see me naked if you care to take the trouble to peep between the newspapers up there.' And she had answered, 'And you can see me from below if you take the trouble.' I wanted desperately to see Edouard with the girl.

I was up there in a second, flat on the floor with my eye stuck to a corner between the crumpled sheets of newspaper. I could see the girl coming out of her bath. She had a nice, round body. Wavy brown hair fell wetly over her face. It wasn't an exciting body, it was simple and healthy and young. But if one likes young girls, then I suppose she did have an exciting body. But she didn't. She was nothing. I knew she was nothing. All one could say about her was that she was there, no more.

Edouard helped her out of the bath. He put a towel around her and kissed her wet face; it was rather touching. Then she dried herself while he watched her. After that, she looked in the mirror and started to make up her face. As she was painting first one eye, then the other, Edouard would bend and kiss her softly. They were two sweet young things.

The shit, I thought. Not because he was with the girl, but because this same sweet, innocent, young thing kissing her like an amorous schoolboy had beaten me and tortured me the day before. He's everything, I thought, good, bad, sweet, a shit. He's every bloody thing.

I hated him. Damn his heartless French soul! She again tried to put on her lipstick, but he kept interrupting to kiss her softly on the side of the mouth. It was really very pretty, but what annoyed me was that she was treating him as a keen young lover. I knew that, sensually speaking, no one in the world (and I had enormous experience) could be more wickedly and exquisitely refined than he. How could this girl treat him like an ardent suitor. She should be at his feet, kissing his hands, his stomach, looking at him and telling him he was the most beautiful man in the world. I nearly laughed out loud that I should decide what she should be doing with him. Damn them both! I must go and make them breakfast.

When we had a second together Edouard said to me, 'I love that girl.'

Putting my arms around him I said, 'That's fine, I love you, too.'

'You're mocking me,' he said. I didn't answer. At least the girl didn't speak French. I couldn't object to her.

'She's good for your English, Edouard.'

Edouard brought her back the following night and that didn't amuse me at all. The morning after the second night the girl left. As it was his day off, I asked him to help in the house. With very bad grace he worked a bit and then he stopped.

'I'm sick of it,' he said. He left and I did not see him again for the rest of the day.

That night he returned with the same girl. I was wild with rage. I couldn't sleep. I didn't even want to sleep. He was not a nice boy . . . but then if he was, he wouldn't be with me. Three nights in a row! I could not let him get away with this.

At eight in the morning I got up to sweep the stairs leading down to the basement. At the end of each stroke I hit the broom against the inside of the banisters making a hell of a noise. Then I started to pull out all the nails from the steps. Ronnie had told me this was his next project for Sunday when he wasn't working and I wanted to save him the trouble. I put all my heart into my work. I bashed and banged for hours. What I couldn't pull out I hammered in. When I had nothing left to hammer, I hammered at nothing. I'd get some reaction out of him. If he had come back at one in the morning and hadn't finished making love until three, then he would be exhausted. He was a lousy waker anyway. He would go mad with the noise.

He shouted out amicably, 'Can't you make a little less noise?'

'If you had done your part of the work, I wouldn't be doing this now.'

'Can't you do it later? I'm with a girl.' he replied, not in the least embarrassed.

'Find somewhere else to stay if it doesn't suit you . . . and Uncle has let your room,' I lied, 'to two Chinese girls . . . so he's not going to sacrifice two rentals for one. Find somewhere you can stay for nothing and have good food and bring in whom you want . . . where no one will disturb Your Excellency.' He took no notice.

I went up to Ronnie and Rachel who were having breakfast quietly and fumed in silence. Rachel put her hand on my shoulder.

'You're dishonest. You only want him near you. You don't care if he works. If you go hammering away like that,' said Ronnie, 'don't tell him you're doing it for the house. Tell him you're hammering to annoy him and the girl because they are irritating you. Tell him the truth.'

I waited till Edouard left his room. I greeted the girl kindly because she was nice and I liked her. To him I said, 'Edouard, I could have fixed the stairs while you were out, but I didn't. I made a noise to wake you and and annoy you, and I hope I succeeded.'

He was good-tempered about it and even smiled. That night again I couldn't sleep. I waited for him to come in, made him his food, and accompanied him down to his room.

'Listen,' he said, 'I'm sick of all this.' By 'all this' he meant my wanting to make love. 'I was amused to start with, but now it bores me. Get out and leave me alone!'

I left the room trying to think what it meant to me. Had it now come to an end? I took two tranquillisers but they didn't help. I walked in the cold, miserable square for another hour and then went back. I had to see him again, I had to touch him, to smell his odour. How long since he had dropped his head on my shoulder? How long?

I went to his room and crept in silently. I put my hands on his head. He was asleep and he didn't move. I passed my hands over his body, his shoulders, his neck. I ran them down the side of his body, down to his feet. I covered him up again and then pulled the sheets out of the bottom of the bed. Edouard was sensitive in the toes. I took them in my hands and started to massage them. Then I put my lips to them. I ran my tongue between his big toe and the next one and I caressed his legs firmly at the same time. He didn't push me away. Then he moved. I could see him clearly by the light of the electric fire. He had risen a little and was leaning on his elbows. I didn't know what he was going to do. I never did. He held his hand to me and said, 'Alors, viens.' I couldn't speak, I closed my eyes and went to him.

Chapter 8

THE NEXT DAY A MESSAGE CAME FROM PARIS THAT KARL WAS coming to London. I knew that he and Edouard had stopped writing to each other. I had spent hours in the room when he wasn't there, looking at his things, touching his letters, his clothes. The room smelled strongly of him by now. It now had a warmth and a personality. Otherwise it might have been a room where they put the dead just before they cart them away. A fire, a lamp, a bright bed cover had warmed it up. With music and the smell of Edouard, it was now a home.

Karl arrived in the morning on a Saturday. I knew he was longing to see Edouard, but Karl wasn't the sap I was. He wasn't going to jump all over him. I went to the bathroom and told him Karl was there. He was pleased. 'J'aime bien Karl. He is the only one who could ever have done anything with me.'

'I'll bring him up,' I said. I told Karl to go to Edouard in his bath. Karl was irritated.

'I'll see him when he comes down.' I went back to tell Edouard. He must have thought it was Karl. He was standing proud and naked in the bath, a welcoming smile on his face. I pretended I hadn't noticed, but I thought of Rachel the first day she had met him. 'There's nothing natural about that boy! Studied. Every single word and movement.'

Seeing it wasn't Karl, Edouard was still determined to have his way. Ten minutes later he came down into the salon wrapped in a towel, stripped to the waist, his face still wet. I thought he looked terrific, but then I couldn't think straight any more. Was he a fake, an actor, or just a boy?

Edouard always behaved decently with me when Karl was about. He did not play us off one against the other and would often let me make love to him when Karl was in town. I encouraged him to accompany Karl and make him enjoy his visit. Karl had been willing to leave Europe because of his feeling for Edouard. I should be kind to him; I knew too well what that was. Karl said he was sharing a room at a smart hotel with an assistant, a young, keen Frenchman not interested in sight-seeing. All he wanted was to get up early, do his work, and go to bed early, Karl told me later.

Karl asked Edouard back to the hotel for a drink, hoping the assistant was out, but he wasn't! Karl suggested the man go and see London—he even said he would put it down to expenses. He insisted the man go out to a night club, but nothing worked. The young man just lay in his bed and told Karl, 'It doesn't disturb me at all for you to have your friends up for a drink—please go ahead.' Edouard was very amused at the whole situation. Karl was drinking, getting nervous and frustrated. He later admitted teasing Karl into believing he might have gone to bed with him. I asked him point blank if he would have, and he said he would not. I wasn't sure. I remembered Karl telling me about an evening he and Edouard had talked late into the night, and how Karl had told me about Edouard complaining that he did not like being with me. When I asked Karl why he was with me, in that case, and not with him, Karl had answered that Edouard was confused.

I didn't find Edouard confused. I thought he was the coolest young man I had ever come across. However, Karl's story worried me. During the evening they spent together Karl had got Edouard to drink and had started on one of those psychological discussions with him. It was Karl, older and more clever, who confused him. Karl had slowly and intricately attacked, contradicted, analysed, proved and overcome, one after another, all the boy's defences, till Edouard had appeared to crumple up before him. He flayed him, called him vain and dishonest, a moral whore, a homosexual hiding his identity. He completely bewildered him that evening.

'I listen to your words like the words of an oracle,' Edouard had said to him. 'You are a wonderful person. I've never met anyone like you. I swear to you. Je suis à genoux devant toi quand tu parles.'

'Then get on your knees, go on, get down on them; I have more to say,' said Karl. And Edouard got down on his knees. Karl had made me promise not to repeat it and I had kept his promise, although I thought it was a dirty trick of Karl's to tell me. I put into Edouard's mind that the whole thing was a plot of Karl's to get Edouard to sleep with him. I did not believe it myself, but I was sick of Karl and everything to do with him. Edouard believed me.

'Yes, I did all those things and I believe Karl when I'm with him, but the moment I'm out of the door, I don't give it another thought.'

Chapter 9

CHRISTMAS WAS AT THE END OF THE MONTH. I WAS ASKED DOWN TO Clarisse and Richard Alderley's country house. Their home was far in the wilds of Wales and they had everything that a Christmas should have—children, horses, dogs and pine trees. Edouard didn't seem very keen on going with me and told me that the bar needed him.

Our relationship continued no better and no worse. There were days when I wanted to stop living, others when I wanted to live forever. I was in an abnormal condition. 'In love' is already abnormal—it's worse at forty for the first time. I had nothing to think about except Edouard. I knew I was being grotesque. I would return to Edouard's room when he was away, touch his clothes, open his old tin box of letters, wander about sniffing, kneel on the floor with my head on his bed. I was unable to pass a shop without thinking, 'Would this be a good colour for his apartment—would he look good in that pullover—should he learn to type on a foreign keyboard or an English one.' At least while I wandered about in front of shop windows I was out of the house.

Rachel begged me to get a job. 'It's not the work you do in the house that's going to help. You must have responsibilities, so many hours a day devoting yourself to something that needs thought. I know, I have been through it. I'm not laughing at you, I am sorry for you. But at least, sometime, you *do* have Edouard for yourself.' She looked suddenly broken, then pulled herself together. 'You are demanding too much. It's bad for you to be in the house all the time, and it's choking him.'

'Let go,' was Ricki's advice. 'He doesn't want you around all the time. Don't go to the bar. They're his friends, his age. What do you think you look like walking with him—you're forty, he's twenty.' I would listen for a day or two and then spoil it. Having an enormous sense of humour, I thought I was not too much of a bore. But then, that was for him to say. I interfered with his life. I would nag him about finding a job for his friend Michel. He had done nothing about collecting his snapshots and trying to earn money modelling. He had not even registered his new address.

One evening at nine o'clock, three hours before he was to come home, I felt lonely. I wanted to be with him so I went down to his room. A light was showing through the slit in the door. I must have left it on earlier when I had cleaned it out. I kicked it open and stood horrified. Edouard and a girl were lying naked on the bed. They were fast asleep with the fire on. They had obviously made love and were knocked out. It was a terrible shock. Not that they were in bed, but that anyone should be in the room at all. I thought the room would be empty. Usually he would tell me if he was bringing a girl home, so that I prepared the place or kept out of the way. Neither of them stirred, so I backed out and went up to my room and took a pill to calm down. It was useless for me to see the thing as it was—boy takes girl to bed. To me it was, How could he have done such a thing without telling me. Why didn't he tell me? I took one of his pullovers and put it next to me, it stank of him. I put my head on it.

I lay there for an hour wishing, hoping, willing him to wake up. Why doesn't he need the bathroom? I thought. He must want to use it. Why doesn't he come up alone, leaving her there? I imagined him with that silent panther step of his walking up to the bathroom. I would call, 'Edouard, I didn't know you were in. Come here and sit on my bed.' He would sit, look at me contemptuously and say he was with some woman, that she was a terrific fuck, that he smelled of woman. 'Look,' he would say and he would come to me and make me smell him and he'd say, 'Go on, take it, take it, it smells of her.' I would twist in pain and pleasure. It was a pretty horrifying day-dream. I lay back exhausted after that. After another hour I heard a noise. I stopped breathing, as I always did when I expected him, to hear him better. It might be anyone, but the step was shifty, animal. It was Edouard!

Where was he going? What did he want? I heard the door open and I couldn't hold back. 'Edouard, come here, I want to see you.' He came in. He was stripped to the waist, wearing a pair of black corduroy trousers. He looked at me in his usual insolent manner.

'What do you want?'

'I want you to come here and sit down for a moment.' He sat on the side of my bed and I held his hands and drew them towards my face.

'Vieux con,' he said. 'You want Edouard, don't you? Come, Edouard, I want to talk to you,' he imitated. 'Edouard, you smell so good,' he continued. 'Yes, I smell good. Look how good I smell.' Looking at me, defiant, outrageous, he slowly unzipped his trousers and crawling up towards me, near my face said, 'Smell it, smell it, it smells of woman! Take it.' I couldn't speak.

After he left I lay there feeling like a trapped animal. Now he was in my mind, reading my thoughts. He had done, step by step, what I had imagined. Hadn't he rung in Paris when I was with the Negro? I was caught like a moth with a needle through its back. He was in my mind, he was in my body. He was destroying me.

Chapter 10

I WAS GLAD WHEN I LEFT A FEW DAYS LATER FOR CLARISSE'S PARTY. She did things in true American fashion. The lights were low and the fire blazed in her long kitchen and I forgot my troubles. The next evening it started again. Karl drank and turned nasty. It wasn't the first time. He accused me of being maudlin, of wasting time with Edouard who couldn't stand me. He continued in front of the other guests. 'I could make him any time I wanted,' he sneered.

'That's unpleasant and unnecessary,' I said. 'Even if it is true, I think you'd better shut up about it.'

Karl was to leave the next evening, to spend the night at Ronnie's. 'No one will be there except Edouard,' I told Clarisse.

'I don't like that man,' she said. 'It's no way to behave when you're in this state, and you are in a state.' She put her hand on my face and kissed me. 'Do you know, dear, that old deaf maid who comes here and washes up every day? You told her all about Edouard. Do you realise this?' It was true I had discussed him. How, I cannot remember, but I know I had. It was getting worse, I must pull myself together. In the meantime I must also warn Edouard.

I telephoned him at the bar. 'Edouard, Karl will be at home tonight when you arrive. Listen, I've been pretty decent about you. I've always told everyone I'm just a dotty man, crazy about you. I've never told them about us, never. Only Karl knows, and Ronnie, since we live in the same house. Don't let me down and don't let yourself down. Karl has said here, in front of mixed company, that he can have you any time he wants to. If he does, that's the end of your reputation.'

'Are you crazy?' answered Edouard.

When I returned to London, Edouard told me what had happened. Karl had returned with champagne and whisky. He had arranged a special dinner. He had tried everything. Edouard had drunk and drunk and left Karl frustrated alone in his room—my room! I felt better.

Before the New Year, Clarisse came to London to prepare for her New Year party. She made an Italian dish called Cotecchino that looks as if it should only be eaten by bawdy merrymakers in the Middle Ages. Black lentils in hot soup, boiled sausages and other meats in one great dish. At two in the morning, when we had finished eating, Clarisse gave me some to take to Edouard.

'He must be with friends, they'll like it. Especially if they are Italian.' At three in the morning I arrived at the bar. It was full. The customers and the barmen were half asleep, but when they saw me come in with a hot dish, Edouard, his friend Lucien, and Giulio who ran the bar, all made a rush for it.

Far from disowning me, Edouard welcomed me with a hug. The boys got animated and Edouard introduced me to a girl as his best friend. Then they all dived into the food, jostling and laughing. I couldn't figure Edouard out. One minute he was ashamed of me, the next he said I was his best friend.

When I was with him later lying on the bed reading a letter from his father, I said, 'Who are you, Edouard? Which is the real you?'

'I don't know,' he said. 'I am to people as they want me.' The father's letter was formal but friendly. He was glad to know that Edouard was with that 'nice couple'—he meant Ronnie and Rachel. He must have thought they were a pair of middle-aged benefactors. He wrote about his own family. How many they were, what each member did. He defended Edouard whom I had accused of laziness. He was not lazy, but lethargic, the father wrote. I chose the moment to offer to buy Edouard a typewriter provided he took a course and learned properly. He wasn't interested.

I had my hand on his forehead, 'It would be a shame, Edouard, to spoil things. I love our friendship. I want to be there for you if you want me, for a long time.' Edouard turned away from me. He choked back a sob, his eyes filled with tears. I couldn't believe it.

I put my hand on them to see if he was really crying and said, 'I didn't know you could. At least you are half human.' I was pleased. He had sobbed for Karl, for what reason I do not know; now he was sobbing for me. Or was he merely tired? Or was he just being what people wanted him to be.

Chapter 11

THE NEXT FEW DAYS SHOWED HIS TEARS MEANT NOTHING. HE BECAME unpleasant, curt, or else he stayed away. It seemed so intentional that I finally told him to get out for good—let him be lonely! I telephoned Nemone Pierce. Her husband was often away and asked if I could stay with her. She was delighted. Rachel and Ronnie were upset that I was leaving, but the next day I packed. They came home to lunch and saw me putting my things into a taxi. They pulled the luggage out of the car and I put it back again. 'I'm leaving and he must too.' I handed them back the house key, but they wouldn't take it.

'No,' Ronnie said. 'This is your home and you may wish to come back when we are away.' I left. My eyes filled with tears.

The next morning I returned and found Edouard sleeping down in his room. I told him that he must go. I took away the last of my belongings and left the house. But I couldn't keep away from him. I returned again the next morning for my mail. I woke him up with a letter and I sat on his bed. I would have given anything for a little gentleness—a hand would have done. He was cold and hard.

'Edouard, you must leave.'

'I'll talk to you about that in a minute,' he said. I accompanied him while he took a long silent bath. I was dying of misery and he was smiling.

'Have you seen Rachel?' he asked.

'No, I haven't. Not since I left the house.'

'She came down to my room yesterday and saw me lying on my bed. I told her I was leaving. She asked me if I had anywhere to go and I said I hadn't. She said she didn't want me to be homeless and that I could stay on.' He turned to me and made a sign with his hands hitting his closed fist into the open palm of his right hand. A sign meaning 'fuck you'.

I could have killed him.

As soon as he left the house to go to work, I telephoned Rachel at her office. How could she let him stay? How could I be her friend if she kept him in the house after I'd gone? Rachel left her work; she met me outside her office. She knew I had been unreasonable, like everyone in love, but she had no idea Edouard had been that callous. She personally felt little for Edouard—he was only here because of me. She would tell him he must leave. She stopped at the bar and told Edouard she regretted that under the circumstances it would impossible for him to stay.

'After all,' she told him, 'you are young and attractive, you have spent nothing all this time. It will do you good to leave.' She now added that maybe later we could both come back. He left and that same day I returned to the house.

During the time I was away and after I returned I saw him seldom, but we still seemed to be friends. He was enthusiastic about his new life. We went to a restaurant together and he told me he was staying with Lucien. Lucien had arrived in England penniless, sleeping in Hyde Park until he found a job and now he was even able to pay for his brother to come over and learn the language.

'Voilà quelqu'un de bien,' Edouard said.

I answered, 'You had a guarantee, free living, clothes, all you needed. Yet you wanted to go on living with my uncle after I left because of you, and you did the same thing again at Rachel and Ronnie's.'

'Je m'en fous. Now I want to stand on my own feet—alone!'

Edouard told me when Lucien went to work in the morning, Edouard would make love with Lucien's girl. Finally the girl had admitted she liked Edouard and they all three slept together.

'Even Lucien is keen on me,' he smiled. Sometimes the other man's girl came to his bed. As far as I could see, he spent most of his time there.

Our relationship was certainly strange. We walked arm in arm in the street. I, who had kicked him out of the house, and he, who couldn't stand me. He would point at some fellow in a café sitting next to us.

'He's interested in what you have to say. Why don't you go for him instead of me?' He was kind to me and he tortured me.

'What am I for you, Edouard? Am I anything at all?'

'Like my parents,' he answered. 'You're there in case I need you. But I don't want to live with *you* any more than I want to live with *them*.'

'What about our plan of saving for a home for you?' I said. 'It needs so little effort and it's worthwhile to have something, one single something, of your own—instead of living like a vagabond.'

'Je m'en fous,' he said. 'Je m'en fous de tout.'

'Will you come to dinner tomorrow?' I asked.

'Bon,' he replied.

'Don't let me down.'

It was awful waiting for that tomorrow to come. But it did come. He came late, sat on my bed and we talked. There was a moment when I thought he wanted to come back—but no, he didn't. I suggested he take a bath. I wanted him to relax, take his clothes off and have a drink. I knew that if he bathed then he'd stay the night and if he stayed, it might mean his return.

'Go on, have a bath, Edouard. I have cooking to do and this way I won't feel I'm wasting time when I could be with you.' He wouldn't.

Now that very morning in the *Daily Express* I had read a curious story that had stuck in my mind.

A woman had been sent to prison for drugging her husband. He was a drunk, and in despair, she had crushed twenty odd tranquillisers and put them into his soup. The husband, tasting a bitter flavour, had poured the soup into another bowl and found sediment at the bottom. He had taken it to be analysed. They recognised the sedative and the woman landed in jail. I had some librium in the bathroom; I would do the same. He wouldn't realise. He would become amiable and stay. He had to stay, he must stay.

I took the tube of librium from the bathroom and put it in my pocket. I went down to the kitchen. I secretly put the librium tablets in my mouth, three or four at a time, chewed them up and spat them into the soup. I tasted it, then I put in more librium. I watched the brew carefully, because I feared it might take away its potency. I could taste nothing particularly foreign in the soup and so, after doctoring it up with peppers and Worcestershire Sauce, I brought it up to him in a bowl. Very nonchalantly I handed it to him saying, 'Here you are, I'm going to prepare the meat. Have a bath first.'

He sat looking at me from the bed, his insolent, hard face staring at me not without humour. 'You have put something in it,' he said, quite sure of what he was saying.

'Oh please, Edouard, shut up. I am very unhappy about you and I want you to change your life and now you're telling me I have concocted something to do with your soup. Don't be childish.'

'Bring me another cup,' he ordered calmly.

'There's a tooth-glass,' I said. 'I go up and down enough for you. What's the matter with you—are you insane?'

Slowly, in front of me, he poured out the soup from the bowl into the tooth-glass. When he had filled it there remained the sediment of the librium in his bowl.

'What's this,' he asked.

'What's what, Edouard?'

'This,' he said, pointing at the sediment.

'I don't really know. I put celery and leeks and all sorts of things in it. That's all. It's hardly my fault if after knowing you six months, you decide I'm poisoning you. Give it to me, you ass.'

Like the food-tasters in Caesar's time I drank half of it. He drank the rest. The sediment remained at the bottom. Nothing happened to either of us . . . and he didn't stay.

I felt it was an omen. I had done everything to keep him and I had failed. I could do nothing to him; he was invulnerable. I was caught. I couldn't fool him or lie to him. Like a loving, tender butterfly, I was pinned, pierced by that callous, French shit. I could never get away—I would never want to get away. Let him stick a needle into my back and stay, holding it as long as I lived.

I was distraught. Rachel came past my room before going to bed. 'It will be alright but maybe you should be apart for a time. He's young, he doesn't care about anything—not about tomorrow, not about a home. He doesn't mind where he sleeps or with whom; if he washes or if he doesn't. You don't know what it is to be young any more, you have forgotten.'

Ronnie said I had treated him wrongly. 'Edouard should know that wherever you are and whatever he does, you stand for "home", you should never let him think you could kick him out. If it's your home, it's his home. He will come back one day. How badly do you want him back?'

Chapter 12

TWO DAYS LATER A LETTER CAME FOR EDOUARD FROM THE FRENCH Consulate. I steamed it open. He hadn't declared his address. I would use this letter. I telephoned him and he was friendly. He even asked me if I would help him buy a pullover. I said I would be delighted and he came round to lunch. I was very unhappy. Several times tears came to my eyes.

After lunch I accompanied him to the underground station, but I was in a state of collapse. As we walked he looked at me and barged into me with his shoulder, playfully. He was trying to encourage me. I couldn't look back. He came up to me again and again, a shoulder and then a look, then he put his arm around me in the middle of the street and said, 'Come on.'

He steadied me and then I pulled myself together and went to the shop with him. The article he wanted to see was a turtleneck sweater in dark bottle green. It was hard and common and I hated it.

'Couldn't I take you somewhere better,' I said. 'It is worth paying anything for something you like.' We went to Liberty's where a sale was on. There was a moss green turtleneck in heavy soft lambswool. The man who served us was enchanting, nothing was too much trouble for him. He gave me a whole selection to choose from.

'I want him to look right in it,' I said.

'Oh, he'd look right in anything.'

He was such a thin man, so unattractive, I felt sorry for him looking at Edouard with such admiration. I sent Edouard down to the dressing-room to try the various sweaters and then I had the madness to say to the man serving, 'Isn't he handsome, that boy?'

'Oh yes,' he said, 'he certainly is.'

The insanity of suddenly discussing Edouard with the man serving us at Liberty's—but then I was mad. Had I not described him to the Welsh daily woman who came to wash Clarisse's dishes? I left and went into the dressing-room.

Edouard wore some sand coloured corduroys and desert boots. He was standing in his singlet and I wanted to devour him. He put the sweater over his head, pulling it down over his face and stretching the end round his narrow hips so that it looked like a taut sack. He was looking at himself in one of the three-faced mirrors and he caught me looking at him. He turned first this way and then that, draping the pullover, twisting right and then left as he moved, his long hair falling over his face. I couldn't run up to him and hug him—I mean, I could have, no one would have seen—but he wouldn't have let me. Looking at me slyly, he said, 'I can understand your being mad about me.' I gave him a whack. He went out wearing the pullover.

'You have time to accompany me to the tailor,' I said to him. 'Will you come?'

'No.'

After he'd gone, I remembered the letter from the Consulate. It would have to wait. The next day was Saturday.

That evening Edouard telephoned me. 'What is it?' I asked.

'I have changed my mind. I have decided to come back and stay with you.'

'I am so happy . . . bless you. When will you come?'

'Tomorrow evening,' he said. I told him I was due to go to Clarisse's and I was certainly not going to let her down.

'Stay in my room,' I said. 'You can't go to your own. They are painting down there. Ring back in ten minutes.' I asked Rachel if that was alright.

'Just tell him I want no girls here this weekend. I want the house to myself. He can bring them when he goes back to his own room.' I told him what Rachel had said.

'Don't let me down, Edouard. Your room will be ready soon and you can do what you like there.' I left for Clarisse's, happy, happy, happy.

I telephoned Rachel the next day and she was in a rage. 'Edouard brought a girl home yesterday,' she said. 'He rang up to ask me and I said he could, though I suppose you gave him the message.'

'Yes,' I said. 'He said he was coming back . . . so he could use my bedroom.' When I returned two days later, I noticed Edouard's things were not yet there. He had not come back to stay—I was right. It was a trick and nothing else. I would get my own back for this.

How dare he play around with my feelings like that and be so rude to Rachel who had never asked one thing from him? He's going to play tricks with me, I'll play tricks with him.

The next day another letter came for him, this time from the Home Office. Again I steamed it open, he had failed to register. God had sent me these letters, no one else but God himself. The time had now come. He was living with Lucien, getting thinner. He was spending his own money. What would he do if he suddenly had no job? He would realise what I was giving him, that it was good not to have to worry about money and food, to bring home the girls he wanted. He didn't want to live for ever with Lucien and other guy's girls, even if they did keep him clean . . . which they did, I noticed with regret. I would think up something, I would fix it. I had to be careful for I didn't want him to lose his job permanently. What could I do now that later I could undo—so to speak? I thought about it very carefully, and, having actually worked it out with paper and pencil, I got busy.

First I telephoned the bar. 'Giulio, a man called today asking for Edouard. I told him the only way to find him was at the bar, your bar. He asked if he was working there and I said, "Oh, I don't know, he always seems to be there". The man asked if he lived with me and I said he had been doing so but he went to the country for a few days. Anyway, Giulio, for God's sake, don't let him work there this evening. You could be fined a hundred pounds if you have someone working there without a permit. Forgive me if I gave your address—the man took me unawares.'

That night I rang Edouard at the bar. They said immediately he wasn't there. I spoke to one of the boys and told him it was I who had found him the job in the first place, not to be afraid to talk to me. 'There are two important letters for Edouard,' I said. 'I opened them both after the man's visit—I must speak to him.' I actually heard Edouard over the telephone refuse to come and talk to me and heard the other man tell him it sounded serious. When he finally came to the phone I told him to leave the bar at once, to go to another bar, anywhere. 'Come here if you like. I have two official letters for you to read immediately. This is serious.'

He came. He asked about the man and he read the letters. He asked what the man looked like, what he had said. I became impatient with him. 'I'm not going to have Rachel and Ronnie dragged into my nonsense having you here when you are not registered. You've troubled us enough. Do you want the police after you? You'd better come back here until things are quiet. By the way, here is another letter,' I said and handed him one from his parents. He was sitting on my bed reading it and he let me read it with him.

Inside there was one for me. They thanked me for my second letter and regretted they didn't know me. They were glad I was looking after their son. I started to weep again. Anything made me weep—a film, a story in the newspapers, anything. I was having a nervous breakdown, that's what it was, a nervous breakdown!

'Edouard, let's leave London for a while. Let's go to the country at Clarisse's—you'll be so happy. You don't know the countryside. You only know Soho. Come and breathe some fresh air—see life from elsewhere than behind a bar. Come on, stay the night and we'll go tomorrow.' He agreed.

As for me—I had got him back. He hadn't a job. He had no work and no money coming in. All he had was me. I would never be able to leave him. He had got me like a butterfly lying flat on its stomach—a pin through its back, right through its back.

Yes, I knew what I must do now. Clarisse would be away the whole Sunday. The house would be empty. I went into Rachel's bathroom and found a long hat pin lying rusting on the window sill. I took it into the kitchen, rubbed all the rust off with Vim and put it over the flame holding it lovingly. I lifted it to my lips and kissed the point. I would do what I had to do Sunday.

That night Edouard slept in the bed next to me, my hand on his head. The separation was over—he was back. I could sleep, I could plan, I could save for a home. I had not lost him after all. One must do what is best, not what is right. Of course it was best to have plotted to have him sacked. I was right. Anyway, what about me? It was him, him, him all the time. Now it was my turn. My conscience was clear. I chose to forget the last conversation I had with Edouard in Soho. With the wind blowing in his hair and in my eyes I had said, 'Everything I do is for you, all for you and only for you.'

He had answered, 'It's for you, not for me. I am your victim.'

We got up at seven-thirty the next morning to take a bus to Paddington Station. There were a few letters in the box as I opened the front door. I stuffed them in my pocket and we ran past the Greek food shop where I had bought things to take to Clarisse. A block of Parmesan cheese, some of that green rocco lettuce, and some okra. I would cook for them all and we would have a wonderful time. The sun would shine and Edouard would fall in love with the country . . . they might even ask him to stay and work there. I would go down weekends. He would be mine again.

As we got into the bus I opened the letters. One was my bank statement. I couldn't quite work out the sum. How was it that I had only that left? It meant that I had to live for the next two months on very little. This was impossible. I couldn't understand. I tried to work out what had happened to the money. But it was not that which was worrying me—it was Edouard. How would I be able to help him now?

'I don't seem to have any money left in the bank,' I said, 'I only have enough for a month. Then what happens?'

He laughed. 'Work,' he said, 'like me!' Then he examined the statement and threw it down. 'Doesn't matter, I have money,' he said. 'It's still in the pot at Ronnie's. There's also the money you gave me in France. You can have it—je m'en fous.'

Chapter 13

WE CAUGHT THE TRAIN. THE JOURNEY WAS DULL. IT WAS NOT particularly beautiful countryside and with his usual French critical sense, Edouard was unimpressed. 'It's not so pretty,' he said.

'It will be later, when we drive from the station to Clarisse's house.' It was bright and sunny when we arrived at Newport. It was market day. Edouard looked better already. It must have been a strain on him too, being on bad terms with me. I hoped so. We took the bus to a small Welsh village where we waited in the square.

There was no one about. Some trees were still green late in January. The houses were of sandy stone and the village full of silent charm. Edouard sat on a pavement hugging his knees. He looked as if he belonged there. He was wearing his new green pullover and his hair had not been cut since his arrival in England three months before. He looked like a creature from the hills. I hoped he would never cut it. His head was too big and it gave him strength. With his square exaggerated jaw bone pulling his skin tight over his cheeks, I thought he was the most exciting man I had ever seen.

Richard arrived in the car and picked us up. He didn't know Edouard but knew more about him than I realised. I had spoken of nothing else, it seems.

Clarisse's house stands on a hill almost entirely surrounded by trees. There is a long drive that dips into a valley where a river full of fish winds slowly down towards the sea. Further up there is a clump of trees through which one can see a glimpse of the white painted house. As one arrives one is greeted by the big, black dog who comes running after the car, covering us with saliva. Before we went into the house I suggested we walk around it. It was a combination of two houses, but it all blended in.

As we walked in through the glass door, I caught a glimpse of us together and it gave me a shock. Ricki had been right when she had said, 'Look at yourself—you're forty, he's twenty.' Edouard looked in perfect harmony with Wales, healthy and tweedy, his shirt open, the hair on his chest showing. I was the one who looked out of place.

The house had not been decorated with a view to impressing visitors. There were the things that Clarisse and Richard had collected in their various travels, some pretty, some ugly, but each told a tale. Their deaf white cat sat on one window-sill after another, haughty and beautiful, taking no notice of anyone. Richard said, 'Unlike most cats she manages to break everything. In Rome, she climbed over our terrace and visited the man next door. The owner happened to be the Japanese Ambassador. The cat would go in and break a knick-knack and steal back to our apartment.' Once Richard caught the cat breaking an antique ash-tray and he had scolded her in front of the dog. The cat realised she'd been insulted. Richard said, 'I saw her climb to the top of the terrace and she was just about to take a leap into space. "Catakiri"—it was obvious! I saved her by telling her she had misunderstood me. She was deaf, after all.' She came straight over to Edouard and whined till he carried her in his arms, where she purred happily.

'Goddam cat,' I said. 'What have you done for Edouard?' Edouard burst out laughing.

After dinner Edouard went to bed. I didn't go and say good-night to him. Richard and Clarisse were spending the following day elsewhere. When we awoke the next morning we were alone in the house. Edouard slept until twelve and I brought him his coffee in bed. I asked him if he liked the place and he said it was wonderful, and he liked Richard and Clarisse too.

Richard said he was a good-looking boy, but Clarisse went on at me for hours! 'You are insane. I'm not blaming you, mind you, we all have insane moments. That is what love is all about. You have given him powers he does not have, you have given him talents he hasn't got. He is an ordinary, healthy boy and you are trying to weigh him down with the heavy hateful burden of your unwanted passion. Of course, you have charm,' she continued, 'of course, he has been amused and touched by you. He probably rather likes you. But, can you think what it can be like for this provincial boy to have an exotic something or other of your age following him like a menacing shadow? He's sick of it. He doesn't want to see tears or hear reproaches. He doesn't care about a home or saving money. He wants to be left alone. Let him alone. He doesn't appreciate what you are. You're a far more valuable person than he will ever be or than he now realises. Give us what you have to give; he doesn't want it. You are suffocating him, and making him despise you. Let him live his life his own way.'

She was right. I must leave him be. And even as I said it to myself I was thinking what I could do to keep him.

We had a lazy breakfast, then we dressed and walked into the fields. It was a brisk, bright winter day. A white pony looked at us from the other side of a fence. 'Edouard, jump on him, ride him—I dare you!' The look of challenge came to his eyes. Smiling, Edouard took a leap and cleared the fence. Then he threw himself on top of the bare pony and they were off. The pony gathered speed with Edouard clinging to his neck, his hair flying. As they neared a dip in the land, the pony gave a gigantic heave and Edouard came toppling off his back and rolled down the hill laughing. He gathered himself together, covered in mud, and tried to mount it again. But the pony wouldn't let him. Tired and happy we returned for lunch.

I fixed Edouard a loaded gin and lemon that went straight to his empty stomach and made him drunk. I gave him raw scallops and a cheese soufflé, followed by a dish I told him they gave to children in England. I don't know whether they did or not, but it was something to say. I wanted everything to amuse and interest him. It was stewed apples covered in strips of bread and butter and brown sugar in the oven. He liked it. Then I took him up to sleep.

'You made me drunk. Think you can do what you want with me?' I didn't answer. I sat him on the bed next to me and pulled a box out of the drawer.

'No, I can't do what I want with you—but you can with me.

You've got me. Tu m'as, n'est ce pas, Edouard?'

'Je t'aurai toujours, I'll always have you where I want you,' he smiled. I was stiff with excitement.

'Alright then—go on—do it, put the needle in—here,' I said, twisting my arm behind me. I handed him the needle from the box. I thought with horror: suppose he kills me.. I didn't care. I wanted to destroy myself. No, I wanted him to destroy me. Holding me down with one hand on my twisted arm he smacked the needle into my back. His palm hit my spine and I came. 'Leave it in,' I said. We both fell asleep. The needle remained.

Next morning on our return to the train with Clarisse, Edouard became sullen. He wouldn't talk. What had I done wrong? I knew he was surly in the morning. If he was not in a friendly mood, I should wait till he was. But why had I to give in to him all the time? Must I always forget myself. I was the one who cared, I must be the one to give in.

Chapter 14

IN THE TRAIN HE LEFT HIS SEAT. HE WOULDN'T SIT IN THE SAME compartment with me. He didn't go away just to have coffee—he left to be rid of me. He was sick of me—sick of my face, my voice. How often had he said to me:

'Even when you're right, tu parles, tu parles, tu parles, et moi—j'en ai marre. I'm sick of it.'

He had no job and he had offered me his savings. Of course, he wouldn't leave me now because he couldn't. But he might. It would be typical of him. He was quite liable to leave without a penny and nowhere to go. He might even do so just to prove how little he cared for me or money. What stops people from leaving each other? Poverty? Loneliness? He wasn't afraid—he was twenty-one, I had not yet corrupted him. There was absolutely nothing to stop him from getting off the train at Paddington Station and never seeing me again. I would crumble. I couldn't let him walk out of my life leaving me broken. Why had he let me love him? Why had he stuck the needle in my back? I knew why—he had done none of these things. I had. One after another, I had done them all—he had obliged, no more.

I tried to think about it objectively. For years I had been getting my own way with people. I had charmed them, tricked them, flattered and seduced them into liking me. Why not Edouard? Why couldn't I charm him? Was I losing my gift, my ability to fascinate and win people over? I needed to test myself. If I could still do it, I would have Edouard back. I had to know.

I looked around the compartment. There were two girls nearby, at the window—they would be easy. Young girls don't usually snub their elders . . . it would be simple to open a conversation with them, pretty little things with that stuff on their eyes. Then there was a long beaked woman opposite me munching an apple . . . biting into the fruit with her false teeth . . . and the colourless girl sitting next to her. I knew how to handle them. On my left was a foreign-looking man. He wouldn't be hard . . . all foreigners in England have complexes. The one I thought might give me trouble was on my right. He was small and quiet. He sat reading a book with a gold cover—an expensive book . . . and he never looked up.

Just as my false-toothed witch bit into her apple again, I interrupted her. 'I'm dying of envy,' I said. 'That wonderful apple . . . I can't resist them. You wouldn't have another to give a suspicious oriental looking gentleman, would you?' She smiled at me, reached into her bag and gave me one. She had fallen for it. I made a few flattering remarks about her . . . and her apples . . . and we began talking. She was with her niece she said.

'Nieces and aunts have *much* better relationships than mother and daughter,' I said. It sounded like the wisdom of the East, but meant nothing at all. She was reading *Madame Bovary*. 'Oh, that's interesting,' I said, pointing to her book. 'My aunt was called Madame Bovary . . . isn't that a coincidence?'

'Was she really?' she asked.

I felt I couldn't lie to anyone so old and proper. 'No, no . . . I really haven't an aunt called that. I have several aunts . . . some that I love and some that I'd love to kill, but none have killed themselves or been asked to a ball . . . and *none* are called Madame Bovary.'

The two girls burst out laughing. The foreign man on my left took no notice, and the man on my right went on reading his expensive book.

'I hope you don't answer me if I talk to you, girls,' I said to the two at the end. 'After all, you look like nice girls and you have no aunt to protect you . . . But I must say,' I said to the one on my side, who had fine dark blue eyes, 'I'm fascinated by your eyes—they are almost violet in colour. Now I have some very good advice I can give you and I will, but not out loud—on a bit of paper here,' I said. 'I'll write it down.' I wrote, 'Anyone with those wonderful eyes shouldn't use hard black mascara but dark blue.' I have no idea if my advice was correct or not.

The man on the left felt something was up as I passed the note over his head. However, he did not look up at me. I looked instead at the book he was reading and saw it was on electronics.

'Oh, dear, the new generation!' I sighed, and smiled at him, looking over his book.

'I have come from my country to study in Cardiff,' he told me. I had always thought of Cardiff as a lost port where half the population was coloured.

'I didn't know anyone went to Cardiff to study!' I said, and for fear of maybe offending some other Welsh people on the train, I added: 'anything so terribly advanced and modern.' I could see he was a foreigner and I wanted to hear him speak a little more to know where he came from by his accent. I didn't want to ask him outright. I never mind people asking me where I come from, but I had discovered that foreigners in England don't like it. So I gave him a chance to go on talking.

'Yes,' he sighed. 'In the old days they came to my country to study and now we go abroad.' He could only be Greek or Egyptian.

'Hellenes?' I asked in Greek.

'Malista, yes,' he said, putting his book down and wanting to talk all the way to London. But I wasn't interested in going further. I had but one idea in my mind—win over everyone in the compartment. But when I discovered he was Greek, I felt obliged to dwell on the beauties of Mykonos and Delos and tell him how I made fish soup the Greek way. Time was getting short. I was worried that in the next hour I might fail to win over the last man—the little one reading the book with the gold cover. I heard that if you stared unblinkingly at someone, they felt it and looked back. He didn't. I glanced at my watch—there wasn't much time left. But I couldn't risk letting it go wrong anywhere. Everything depended on him—that was what my test was for. God knows, he could have looked up a dozen times and shown his co-operation. He hadn't stirred—his nose was stuck in that gold covered book. It was a barrier between us, that expensive, orderly looking volume he was so engrossed in. There must be some way, some disarming gesture that he couldn't escape. I would touch him, that's what I would do! I'd show Edouard!

I put my hand on his sleeve and said, 'Won't you please join us! We are having fun. I see you don't need us, but we do need you.' After giving me a surprised look, he was won over by my mad offer. He closed his book, and as he did so I said, 'Don't, you'll lose your place and it is such an expensive book, too. Being half oriental, I am particularly impressed by anything gold and the cover is so splendid. Thank goodness it isn't on electronics, like the other man's. At least I'll be able to understand what I read over your shoulder!' Then I proceeded to introduce him to everyone in the compartment. 'This is Aunt,' I said. 'This is her niece, and the student from Greece . . .' I couldn't go on; it was so insane, and the whole compartment was giggling.

'And you must be?' I said, and then I thought deeply and seriously: fine hands, small, bright, intellectual looking, a cultured voice. What could he be? 'You're an anaesthetist!' Again they all laughed.

When it was quiet again, he said, 'It's very funny that you should think I'm an anaesthetist. As a matter of fact, I am of the medical profession.'

'So I was right?'

'Half right. Actually, I am a doctor.'

'Not a psychiatrist?' I asked hopefully.

'I'm afraid not.'

'Oh dear,' I said. 'I am in such trouble. I have a psychosomatic problem. Wouldn't it have been wonderful if you had been just the man I needed and you had been able to arrange it in a minute on the train?'

A month ago I had noticed on the end of my nose a slight red point. It was not a pimple, for it had no head to it . . . neither was it a scar, nor a boil. I didn't know what it was, and I would stare at it in the mirror. If I pressed it, it would disappear, but when I looked again it was back. Once I stuck a needle into the point and it bled profusely, out of all proportion to its insignificant size. I thought I had cured it, but when it healed and the scab formed and fell, the red patch was still there. However, one could hardly see it, and certainly no one on the train had noticed it. 'I have a psychological spot on my nose,' I said, 'could you advise me how to get rid of it?'

The doctor was amused and asked me where it was. 'It isn't always very visible,' I said. 'I went to a doctor in Paris and he put an electric needle into the last one I had, it went bzz, bzz, and a scab formed and a week later there was nothing left. What can I do about this one—I know no doctors in England.'

'It's very easy,' he said. 'Go to any doctor and get on his panel. There's free medical treatment here now. He'll send you to a hospital and they do it for you free.'

'But that means hanging around after first going to a doctor and then trying to get in early before the queue, an endless affair for such a trivial thing. Is there no way of avoiding all that?'

'Well, yes,' he hesitated. 'You could go to any hospital straight to the casualty ward. There would be no waiting.'

'Now I'm pretty outrageous, I know, but I can't see myself pushing past an internal haemorrhage and a crushed knee, pointing at the psychological pimple on my nose and saying "Help." I mean—how could I? You have spoilt everything for me, doctor. I couldn't do that. How would you receive me if you were the doctor on duty?'

'It's a shame I'm between hospitals,' he said. 'It's such a simple thing. All one has to do is cauterise it. One could do it oneself!'

'How,' I said, turning on him and looking at him like a public prosecutor.

'Well . . . I could do it.'

'Alright, then do it. Do it now, right away, at once!'

'I can't do it here.'

'Yes, you can—can't he, all of you?'

I looked round at the others and they looked delighted. 'What do you need to make a good job of it, doctor?'

'You put something red hot on it. It will dry up and leave no mark.'

'How do you propose to do that?'

He smiled at me and he felt in his lapel for a pin. After that he took out a cigarette and put the pin through it. I had no idea what he was doing. He lit his cigarette lighter and put the flame below the pin. This he held for a minute until the pin was red hot. I got nearer to him, spellbound by the preparation. Then he grabbed my nose and plunged the red hot thing into the psychological spot. There was a psscht, a smell of burning flesh and the whole thing was over.

I thanked him profusely for saving me money, for restoring my self-confidence, for making me feel clean and no longer a leper. Then I had a thought. 'What happens, doctor, if you've made a hole in my nose? How will I ever find you and . . . how will I ever be able to fill it and with what?'

I looked towards the corridor. Edouard had returned and was watching through the window. The sullen face that had left an hour ago had disappeared. The hardness had gone, leaving a wry smile. He helped me out of the train—I needed it. He put his arm through mine, muttering 'Sacré Jo!' I was saved.

Chapter 15

I REALISED THAT IF EDOUARD WAS NICE TO ME I COULD DO ANYTHING. I was worried about my financial situation and I felt awful about using his savings, so I thought I'd work! That sounds normal enough—but for me, who had never worked, it wasn't.

It was easy for me to borrow money, since sums would always arrive without reason from family funds. I asked Edouard if he would like me to work at the Voyous Bar and he said that if I did he would leave!

'But you're not working there now,' I said. 'Why can't I take your place temporarily?'

I suggested he take a course in typewriting. 'It will be useful to you if you're in some company in the Sahara or working for Air France.'

'Why Air France?' he asked.

'I suppose you will get sick of looking like a caveman, although I am mad about the way you look now. Besides you'd look so handsome in that blue uniform,' I replied.

'Shut up,' he said good-naturedly.

Then unexpectedly I received a large cheque from home. I immediately wrote to my bank in Switzerland asking that they write to the English authorities to inform them that they would be sending Edouard a cheque each month. He would have an income. I took him to the bank and made him open an account for himself. When he came out, he walked differently.

'Edouard,' I said. 'You look different. How do you feel?'

'Different,' he said. We walked arm in arm to his school and I left him there.

'With this letter from the bank you can go to Giulio at the Voyous, and you are OK as far as the authorities are concerned. You have money coming officially and you are just helping out at the bar if they ever catch you.' That night they took him on again and he was happy.

He had taken that girl back to *my* room at Rachel's because his room had been full of workmen's tools. Now it was empty again and he was able to move back in. Two new beds had been put into my own room. The floor had been polished and the whole house looked better. The basement still had to be attended to, the shutters in Edouard's room needed changing. The door to his bedroom would have to be changed too. It had a split in it. One could almost see through it. Yes . . . one could almost see through it. But his bed was around the side, on the same side as the door. I would see nothing. Rather than wait for him to demand his room back, I prepared it and put the bed in a different place. And he could sleep with me too. I said, 'Stay with me now, Edouard. Your room is always ready. When you want to bring a girl home, then you go downstairs.' These were the happy days when I would lie in bed waiting for Edouard . . . asleep or pretending to be asleep. He would come in with his silent rubber shoes, creep up to my bed and sit on the edge of it, immobile. Sometimes I really was asleep; most of the time I only pretended. Slowly he would edge towards me and then he would lay his forehead on my shoulder. I would wake up with a start. 'God, how I love you,' I would say.

Sometimes Edouard would say, 'Cesses ton cinéma'—stop your play-acting. Or sometimes he would say simply, 'Je sais.'

But it only lasted for about ten days. I had been nagging Edouard about helping his friend Michel to come to England. Michel had written occasionally—I had read the letters—and just lately he had written complaining that Edouard was not doing his best for him. On that particular morning I had gone to the door to get the post and I saw a letter addressed to Michel in Edouard's handwriting. He had sent it to the wrong address and it had been returned.

I knew it was madness to read it, dangerous too. But it didn't stop me. I steamed it open and took it to the basement. It was Edouard's letter alright, written in tiresome slang.

'Alors, vieux con . . . Don't pester me about coming over, leave it all to me. Stay till summer when you get your bonus. You need about fifty pounds to get here. I'll get you a job and we'll have a hell of a time—we'll show 'em. I have London taped. The Queer has got me a place that doesn't cost anything. To be a student, you have to prove that you're receiving money. I fixed it with him. He sends me money from his bank in Switzerland to show I'm receiving it, then I give it back. Who needs his money?'

I steadied myself against the wall. I couldn't believe it. I was abject. Only a few moments ago I lay in his arms. He had said, 'You'll always be my friend; you have taught me to love and to be clean'—and now this! He had been sleeping in my room. He didn't have to, his bed was ready downstairs. Why then this letter? He should have left me, left the house.

And what did Michel think? Why hadn't Edouard brought him over yet? Either Michel knew the truth and he and Edouard were whores, or else Michel should be outraged by such a letter—if he were a decent boy. I held it but I couldn't bear to look at it. I turned my head away. I thought of those tarts who went with fat old men. 'I don't mind if you're bald, I think you're lovely.' The old men believed them. This was not exactly the same, but it was not exactly different either. That I should have Edouard close to me at night planning tomorrow, talking of a family, taking him to the doctor, or that he should have given me money, his money, all he had in the world and then written this rotten letter. None of it made sense.

Ronnie saw me with my long, sad face at breakfast. 'What's happened now?' I told him. He looked at me with those intelligent blue eyes of his. 'You're naughty. Don't you know one doesn't open letters and if one does one pays for it?'

'Oh Ronnie, I am so terribly hurt. Look at this.' He read it in front of me.

'It's not very nice. He should never have written it, but it doesn't mean anything. It's a defence young people put up to show each other how tough they are. You are dealing with a generation whose greatest proof of being contemporary is to say, "Je m'en fous". Edouard wouldn't be with you if he didn't like you. A handsome boy of that age could be with someone else, with a girl!'

'But he couldn't, Ronnie. He is with me because it suits him. Who else would feed him and give him what he wants and let him go to bed with whom he wants?'

'They don't care at that age,' Ronnie said. 'They'll sleep anywhere, with anyone. They'll pay, they'll get paid. He is fond of you, otherwise how could he stand being near you?' I wanted to say I didn't think he could, but what about these last nights? He could have turned away from me. He didn't.

'What shall I do?'

'Nothing, forget about it.'

Not satisfied with Ronnie's good counsel, I told Ricki what I'd done.

'If you are foolish enough to read a letter that isn't yours,' she said, 'don't be more foolish and act on it. Forget it.' These two people were my friends—they knew the torment I was going through. They both gave me the same advice.

I went to our room. Edouard was lying asleep. I looked at his face, at the face I had looked at with such devotion for nearly six months now, and saw nothing but evil in it. Callous, cruel, caddish! I took both pages of the letter and stuck them up against the wall opposite his bed and woke him up for some coffee.

'Special breakfast for my best friend,' I said. 'Special day today. Today is friendship day. Today is the day everyone sends messages and presents to their friends. What are you going to give me? I mean, what can I do for you? I keep forgetting you are my friend . . . I'm not yours.' I went on: 'Edouard, I am so dotty this morning —imagine what happened to me. I had an awful dream. I dreamt Michel wrote to me. You know, your friend Michel in Paris. He wrote to me, can you imagine? His letter said: "Dear Jo—for some months now I have been suspicious about Edouard's intentions to help me get a job in England. Today, after telling me he lived with you as your trusted and intimate friend, I get a letter from him saying he can fix things up for me through you, the imbecile Queer whom he despises. When I first got the letter, I was excited about coming to London. Then I thought about it carefully. I decided I couldn't trust anyone that false. Could you arrange something for me. I don't want to come through Edouard anymore." '

Edouard didn't answer. Slowly he got out of bed and put on his dressing gown. Then he looked at me.

'What's the matter with you?' he asked.

'Look at my awful dream.' I pointed to the letter, which I had stuck on the wall. Then I burst out laughing. 'Don't be worried, it's not as bad as you think. I'll tell you what happened. This morning while you were asleep I went to a séance—one of those things with mediums, and we all laid our hands on the table and then one of the mediums asked for a pen and she wrote out this letter. Of course, it's not your letter.'

Edouard showed no sign of defeat, but he was so completely caught, there was nothing he could do. Nor could he understand what had happened. How did his letter get into my hands? Had Michel really sent it? Had he really been betrayed? He said, 'I don't believe Michel could have done this.'

'I don't believe you could have either, yet you did, didn't you? Or is it just the handwriting of the medium?'

Edouard was beaten. But his sense of logic made him ask for the envelope in which the letter had arrived.

'Maybe the dustbin,' I said. He went down to the yard to look. 'It's empty,' he said when he came back.

'It's always emptied at nine o'clock in the morning,' I said. 'But what does it matter, Edouard? I know what you are. I shall write to Michel myself and tell him the truth—you don't mind, do you?' So I sat at the table and wrote Michel the whole truth about my relationship with Edouard. I told him I didn't know what Edouard was, that he had given me his own money once, that he had refused presents; so if he was with me, either he was a very modest whore, or maybe even a queer who wouldn't admit it!

'I will post it,' said Edouard, as I put it into an envelope lying on the table.

'You wouldn't dare.' I went to the bathroom just to see what he might do to save himself.

When I returned, he had put a stamp on the envelope I had prepared. 'I don't mind Michel receiving this,' he said. 'If he could betray me to you, then I want no more to do with him.'

'Wait a minute,' I said, 'I shall post it.'

'Alright,' he said, 'you post it.' I was convinced he had fooled me. He couldn't face my sending that to Michel. 'Thank you for trusting me, Edouard, like I trust you!' As I said this, I opened the closed, stamped envelope and pulled out what was inside. Edouard had stolen my letter and changed it for a plain piece of paper. 'You really have lost the day, haven't you, you little shit! Now get out. Go to your bar and I'll tell you later what I have decided to do about it.' I lay in a hot bath trying to relax. Now I had to end it.

The following evening I rang Edouard at the Voyous. 'How are you?' I asked.

'Not so hot.' He sounded ashamed. I hated to see him suffer. I had wanted to show I could get my own back but I did not want to worry him further.

'The letter you sent to Michel came back and I opened it. You shouldn't write those things and if you do, you shouldn't stay.' He was nice to me for the next few days.

At night I used to wait for him with a pullover of his on my pillow. But one evening when I was about to go to sleep, I didn't see one about and went to find one. I opened his trunk. But that was no use. I had trained him never to put away anything dirty. I panicked. How could I go to sleep without something smelling of Edouard? I went to the basement where I had hung the washing. I might have left something unwashed, something that smelled. Everything was out on the line. I returned to the room, undone. I went to the dining-room where Ronnie and Rachel were sitting quietly.

'Whatever's the matter?' asked Rachel. 'You have been running up and down stairs. What are you looking for?'

'A pullover of Edouard's,' I said. 'There isn't a dirty one left. I always take one to bed with me.' Rachel and Ronnie said nothing. They looked at each other and then at me.

'Come here, darling,' said Rachel, and I went and knelt on the floor where she was sitting. 'There, there,' she said, patting me on the head. 'He'll be back in two hours and you can have the real thing.' Then we laughed uncontrollably, all three of us.

Chapter 16

THE FOLLOWING AFTERNOON WAS A SUNDAY. I HAD AN APPOINTMENT with a beautiful young couple. He was a Brazilian student in London, she was from Paris. We had nothing to do, so I suggested spending the afternoon in Edouard's bar. There was not a soul on the streets and even the bar was empty; Edouard was dishevelled and bored, holding hands with a sharp-faced, black-haired girl. Not pretty—but interesting.

While we were talking, choosing records and wandering around the bar, Edouard came over and whispered, 'I'm bringing her home tonight; prepare the room downstairs.'

'Of course,' I said. I minded, but not much. I had always asked him at whatever time he came home, to come in and see me and he always had. I knew it bored him, so I said, 'Don't bother to come by tonight.' I didn't mind who he slept with—I only minded not being sure of him. This was his power.

I came home to prepare his room. I moved the bed opposite the entrance door. Then I closed the shutters and looked from the outside to see if I could see inside. I couldn't. Then I looked through a slit in the middle of the door panel. I couldn't see a thing. I went to the kitchen and got a knife, a broom, and a dustpan. I couldn't decide whether to stick the knife through from the outside or the inside. I was afraid Edouard might notice a difference. I started from the inside, running the knife up and down a dozen times. Then I did the same thing from the outside. The split seemed unchanged, but one could see clearly through.

When that was finished I returned the things to the kitchen. Ronnie was sitting with Rachel.

'What have you been up to?' he asked.

'Nothing,' I said, 'just preparing Edouard's room.'

'Don't tell us that. We're your friends, and we're sharp, you're up to no good for sure.'

'I'll tell you tomorrow,' I said.

'See that you don't regret it,' said Ronnie.

I went to bed. I had a moment of shame and fear. What if the lovers catch me? What if they hear me going down the stairs. They wouldn't catch me—I would go through the basement entrance. That would make no noise at all. I left the basement door open and went to take a sleeping pill. Then I thought, maybe she won't come, why should I be asleep when Edouard returns. I shan't take it. Then again, if she does come and it bothers me, I can always take it then.

It ended as usual, by my not breathing from midnight until a quarter to one when I heard footsteps. There was no question of my taking a pill. What was I thinking about?—I had prepared everything to see them making love. I wanted to see what Edouard was like when he really cared for someone.

Half an hour later, I walked silently down to the ground floor, stretching my neck out over the railings going down to the basement and listened. I heard whispering and footsteps. Edouard was leaving the new bathroom downstairs and returning to his room. I then went back, dressed, went out of the front door and hurried to the back door. This saved me creeping down that creaky staircase to Edouard's room. The door had been locked in the meantime, damn it! Why hadn't I waited till evening to unlock it? I stood on those stairs in the back entrance on my left foot and gave myself a sharp angry kick on the behind with the right. I remember doing it.

Now I had to go back, change into my pyjamas, and creep down the creaky indoor staircase.

The journey down was agony. I couldn't tell which step was going to creak so I put each foot gingerly down. The less steps I used, the less chance of my making a noise. I did every third step, holding my breath. I felt I had spent all those last months holding it. It must have taken hours. It felt it! I had to see them, Edouard making love to that woman. I had to. It was a matter of life and death.

It was hardly a yard to the door now, I could see the light coming through the crack. Oh God! Suppose Edouard had moved the bed! He was so cunning, he always got the better of me. Please God, see that it's alright—that he hasn't moved it or covered the crack. Please, please . . . I put my hands to my head. I wanted God, God I didn't believe in—to help me spy on the man I loved while he was fucking. I don't care. I don't care. I must see him, see him take that woman, lie on her, love her, hurt her, make her weep.

The crack was gaping at me, it almost had an expression. I bent my head down. Nothing had been moved. I could see it all. They were lying in bed. They hadn't started yet. 'Viens, come on,' I heard. Then he repeated it more purposefully, 'Viens.' He put his arms round her shoulders and leaned on her till he had folded her down onto her back. I think he was kissing her—I don't know. I saw only the nape of his neck with the long, falling untidy hair. Then he pulled up the bedclothes with his right hand and told her to get inside. After that I couldn't see him. She was lying on her back groaning. Her eyes were closed and she was giving herself up to her pleasure.

I wasn't curious to see what was going on in order to steal from them and I didn't seem to cheat on her in any way, I wanted only to be sure she was enjoying him—that he wasn't wasting himself on her. I didn't want him to give one single second of himself to some silly girl—like the last one. This one might appreciate him. She was more mature.

Her arms were thin and it gave her a more intense, desperate quality than if she had been a fat healthy fuck.

During these moments I think he must have been kissing her breasts. I felt he was, but he was hidden under the sheets. Occasionally, she would bring her arm down and under the bedclothes and then out again. I wanted to move, to change my position. I no longer knew how long I had been there. My back and my neck ached, I felt a draught. Carefully and silently I altered my position. Then I took a handkerchief from my pocket and used it as a cushion between my forehead and the door, so I could lean against it with comfort. There were a few creaks—the floor, the door, my neck, but the lovers were too absorbed to hear.

Then he threw off the covers and turned over on top of her. She kept her eyes closed and he started to kiss her, but his kisses were harsh. He kissed her along the side of her face, roughly, without affection. His lips did not make the noise of a kiss, he did not close them as he ran his half-open mouth up the side of her face, to her ear and down to her neck. He veered over towards her and gave her a quick, hard brush on the mouth with his own.

He was handsome making love. His profile was pure, his body more feline than ever. His shoulders were hunched and round and the small of his back curved in, his big legs hung heavily from his small, tight ass. Occasionally she put her arms around him, but mostly she was passive, entirely passive.

Then he separated her legs and penetrated her. He remained there, quite still, not moving at all. Then he started, but with such speed I found it unbelievable and he went on, frantically, endlessly. While on top of her, he left no part of her body free. His hands ran up and down from her waist to her hips to her buttocks and down to her thighs and back. He never left any part of her unattended. When she came she gave a pathetic cry, almost doubled right up, and then fell back helpless and exhausted. A second later he came. I waited for this. I never knew how real or how affected it was, but when he came he made a noise such as I have never heard, startling. I waited for it and there it was, a terrifying roar of agony, pain, death. Then he collapsed on her, empty, drained, finished.

I got to my feet when he began to move and I made my way to the top of the stairs. Edouard came to the door. I tiptoed down towards him—he looked furiously at me. I lifted my hand so that he didn't speak. He came nearer and when he was near enough to hit me, which was the same distance as for me to kiss him, he whispered angrily, 'What are you doing here?' I said nothing. What could I say? He had caught me. But I wanted to say, 'I watched it, all of it. You were extraordinary. I've never seen anything like it You were wonderful.' Instead I turned from him and walked away back to my room.

I lay on the bed and recalled the whole scene. Then I turned on to my stomach and tried to move as quickly, as violently as he had when he was on her. It was impossible. I didn't put it down to my greater age nor my heavier body, but to the magic of Edouard. In the realms of love he must be unique, that's all.

When I came down to breakfast next morning only Ronnie was there, Rachel had left for work. He stared at me knowingly, waiting for some confession.

'I saw it all, Ronnie. Everything. I never saw a man make such love. He was touching her everywhere at the same time. His hands were running up and down her thighs and his arms seemed all round her and he never left any part of her uncared for, it was . . .'

'So that's what you were up to,' he laughed. 'Never seen a couple making love without them knowing it? It's always marvellous when it's someone else! Does Edouard know? He'll say he did.'

I left Ronnie for the bedroom where Edouard had come to change after the girl had gone. 'Edouard, did you know I have watched you making love?'

'Of course.'

He must be in love with her. He's going to leave me to live with her. He couldn't be that passionate if he wasn't in love. 'Are you in love with her?'

'Cette connasse. Silly bitch, I shan't go to bed with her again.'

Chapter 17

THE REST OF OUR STAY AT RONNIE'S PASSED WITHOUT INCIDENT except for one evening when Edouard and I were both in a wonderful mood, laughing and friendly. It was his night off and he came home early. I wanted games with Edouard and he wanted peace. He didn't really want peace—I think he wanted me to annoy him so he could play his part. In any case, I wouldn't leave him alone, I kept playing with his hair. There is such a huge difference between irritation and pretended irritation that when Edouard said, 'Take your hand away,' I knew it was all going to be a game. I would see how far it went. It started with a bit of wrestling around the room, but that didn't keep me quiet so he decided he would torture me.

I made a feeble attempt to resist. I hated beating him at anything. 'I'm going to tie you to your bed so you can't annoy me any more,' he said. It was a friendly farce, and it lasted till I was firmly tied to the bed, a leg to each side. My hands were tied to the top of the bed but they were able to move, like a dog with a long rope attached to its neck.

First he blindfolded me then he gagged me. When I was firmly tied, down he came over to me, bared my eyes and shone Ronnie's steel lamp right into them. It was painful and humiliating and I shut them hard but he forced the lids open and made me glare into the light. I wanted the game to go on forever. We were together, Edouard and I, no one else existed.

We had been playing around for a time, when abruptly, he stopped. 'J'en ai assez de ce cinéma,' he said. Covering me up, he turned the light out and went to bed, lighting a cigarette as he always did last thing before going to sleep.

I wriggled round and found that although I could do nothing with the rest of me, my left hand was free enough to reach out to his bed. Instead of merely moving his bed away, he said, 'Shut up or I'll burn your hand.' I held onto the sheets of his bed and continued my game. Edouard took a puff from his cigarette so he could feel its warmth and it excited me.

'He'll never do it,' I said to myself, but I knew he might. He might do anything, so I went on pulling at his sheets. He let some ash drop and some hairs on my hand sizzled. I remember I was smiling. He told me to let go, but I wouldn't. He pressed the thing into my hand. A surge of something like a sea of snow came over me, went up through my head blocking my ears. It was like being anaesthetised.

'I won't let go, I won't,' I groaned through my gag and he pressed it out on my hand. I only remember saying, 'I love you.' Then he untied me and let me go. I slept with my hand in his, the one he burned. I have the scar today.

Chapter 18

FEBRUARY WAS OVER. I HAD MISSED CARNIVAL IN RIO. HOW LITTLE it mattered. Another country, another journey, another sensation. I had found what I wanted. Now to start saving for Edouard's apartment. Maybe with a little capital his father could do some advantageous thing for him. No, I must do it myself. I had furniture in storage. I would get the flat and decorate it. Edouard was a kid and had no taste and he wasn't going to live there right away. At last! Something to live for, someone to live for, some reason to wait for each day. I felt warm and fulfilled. I had a responsibility.

Rachel's relations were arriving from abroad, and after all these months at her home I felt it was time to make a move. I missed my car and I missed Paris. Either I could return to Paris on good terms with Edouard and plan for the future, or stay with him in London.

I put it to him. 'I would like to take a small apartment I have been offered. Does it interest you? There are two rooms. I will try to arrange them so that you can bring home whom you will. It will cost you nothing. On the other hand, if you want to be alone, then I shall go to Paris and you can come and see me now and then. Of course I prefer staying here with you. What do you think?'

He thought for a minute and agreed, 'Take it,' he said. I said no more to him. Overjoyed I went to work on it the following day. I worked so well and so quickly—nothing was too much trouble—no hour was too late. The location was good. The flat had no telephone, but I could see to that and there was a bath with boiling water on the landing.

The urgency with which I explained the necessity of having the phone installed when I was with the telephone company resulted in it being ready within three days. Unheard of in London at that time.

I was ecstatic. 'Edouard, all we need now is to do a little more work on the apartment and then we can move in.'

'That's your affair,' he said. 'I've my job and school.'

'I will need you to move some furniture from Ricki's, the rest I can do myself. All I really need from you is your enthusiasm!'

I had started by ripping up the linoleum. Each morning I'd change into overalls, scrape the floor with sandpaper and a wire brush. Then I would scrub it all with soap. I felt strong and light-hearted. It had all been worthwhile—the drama, the agony, the madness. He would be with me at last.

I started by buying sheets for him. My idea was to get things that would later be of use in his new apartment in Paris. When they arrived I took them back and changed them for double sheets. One day he would marry. These sheets were to be used for him and me now, and later? For him and his wife? Edouard was right, what I did for him was for me, and for me alone.

I had decided to move into the apartment the following evening. Edouard was to be free then and I needed his help. Nemone had already driven us to Ricki's to borrow a bed and a table. Nem had been so sweet to me, seeing me happy.

'I don't dislike that French frog,' she said. 'He's a disgruntled thing not unlike my own husband, but I see what you mean. He has something, in an earthy, primitive way.'

We moved Edouard's stuff into Nemone's van and up to the new apartment. It was a March day, of sudden warmth after the long winter. For me it was the dawn after the long ordeal of darkness.

'Get a move on,' Nemone shouted. 'Stop looking at the French oaf.'

We seemed to have amassed so much stuff between us. I could never make it alone and why should I? He was going to live there, it was to be his home. 'I have the key for you,' I had said to him the previous evening and he had taken it greedily out of my hand, saying he would take a girl there that night. It was our home! Couldn't he wait till I was settled there first. It was mean and tactless.

He promised to be at Ronnie's the following evening at seven to help me move. I rang the bar at half-past six and asked if Edouard was there. He came to the phone and said he couldn't help, he was working. It didn't matter. In six hours he would be home to stay. I was no longer alone.

At midnight I thought of telephoning to ask if all was well, but why bother him? He would come alright, I would wait. So I waited. By one o'clock he hadn't appeared. There were times he arrived at Ronnie's as late as one o'clock, besides, the new flat was further away. By half-past one he had not come. The table was set, the food was waiting, everything was ready. I had even put flowers in a vase to make the place less bare and the person it was all for wasn't there. How could anyone be so callous? He knew I was in an abnormal state of mind. He must have found some new adventure. If he was a friend, he would put off his adventure. This was our evening, our new home. I had done my best to make it warm and happy. And now he hadn't appeared.

He knew where the place was, and even if he didn't, he knew the telephone number. He could have taken a taxi, he could have told me he wasn't coming. He hadn't helped me move and now he hadn't even come.

I twisted and turned all through the night and when the morning came I was still without news of him. I was in all the next morning, and still no news. I refused to believe something had happened to him. Things don't happen to people, they just don't—not those things. I supposed I could contact him at the bar. I telephoned. No, they hadn't seen him. They didn't expect him till five o'clock that afternoon. So I just waited. At five-past five I telephoned again.

Edouard answered me cool as can be. 'You're alive, Edouard? What happened to you?'

'I lost your number,' he said.

'Then why didn't you come?'

'Oh well, I met someone and I . . .' I hung up on him. He rang back.

'Fuck off, Edouard, I've worked at this place for a week, I did it all for you, now I'm sick of you.'

'I'm coming this evening,' he said.

'No you're not, I've had it—I can't go on. Don't come.' I rang off. I wasn't depressed at that moment. At ten o'clock I returned home after having stayed out as long as possible. The telephone rang—it was Edouard.

'I'm coming this evening,' he said.

'I don't want you to.'

'I want to come,' he said.

'Well I don't want you to.' But I wanted him then, later, at midnight, anywhere, any time, always. I lay on my bed tired, sore, aching. He would come, he couldn't not come now. I was breaking down, slowly breaking down.

At one o'clock, I heard the squeak of rubber shoes on the linoleum of the hall that led to the door of the flat. I didn't speak when he knocked at the door. I didn't move—I'd keep him worrying—if he was worrying. But I didn't think he was. He'd find another bed, other arms. I opened the door and he stared at me, a smile on his face. I put my arms around him. 'I guess it will go on this way till—till it stops.'

He was tender with me. I put him to bed and laid my head on his chest till he fell asleep. I didn't want to sleep. I wanted to enjoy every second with him.

He slept till midday when I made him lunch and sent him off to work. 'See you tonight,' he said. I put all his things out. His trunk with the pullovers I had bought him was in the corner. His blazer we had bought the first day was hanging in the cupboard. 'Home,' I thought.

That night he returned. He was tired and I let him sleep. In the morning when I came to him he didn't push me away. It was ten o'clock by then. He looked at the window and asked me why there were no curtains. 'I will get some,' I said. 'Go back to sleep.' I went down the King's Road, bought some material, came home, measured the window with a piece of string and started to sew. Two hours later they were hanging. Edouard lay fast asleep.

I woke him up slowly and gave him breakfast. 'Something is different,' he said.

'You complained there were no curtains,' I said, 'but you made a mistake, there are.' He looked around, smiled, and put his hand on my head.

'Sacré Jo,' he said, and went to his bath. He came back, laid on the bed and we talked.

'I'm going to Ronnie's to get the mail. I'll be back in an hour—wait for me.' I must have been singing as I got into the underground at Sloane Square. An elderly man with a nice face spoke to me.

'So nice to hear someone singing: you must be happy.'

'Yes,' I said, 'I am, and I hope you feel like singing too.'

At Mornington Crescent Underground Station the woman selling flowers at the corner smiled at me, and said, 'You're 'appy, aren't you?'

'Yes, I am.'

''Ave a flower, dear,' she said, and handed me one. I was happy, humble, afraid. It had all been worth it. Rachel had always said if I waited enough and cared enough—or was it Ronnie who said that, or did I say it myself, or did I just hope it. Anyway it was true. This is where one life ends and another begins. I had hated my childhood, I felt life had been a series of betrayals, frustrations and lack of love. If that was the price for getting this at forty, it was worth it.

I got back home and opened the door. There was no sound, a note on the bed said, 'Back in half-an-hour, Edouard.' This meant he would be back any moment. I had hoped to find him in, but what matter? In today, or now, or tomorrow, he was living with me! I looked round the room. The bed wasn't made, but there was a strange look about the place, something was different. The corner! The corner where the trunk was—the trunk with the pullovers in it—where was it? He had moved it, it wasn't anywhere. The empty corner looked back at me. I felt sick. I couldn't look at it and I couldn't look away from it. I looked in the cupboard. His blazer was there, and his shoes. What about the other valise? I went into the little room. It was gone too. Edouard had gone—he had gone. Why had he left a note saying he was returning? I started to shake, I sank to the ground for a second, then took a deep breath and pulled myself together. Wait, calm down, wait, He's coming back.

When he does return, be quiet, take it easy, relax, don't moan and groan. Other people's tears are such a bore. Be cool, play it right! Then Edouard knocked at the door.

I held my hand out to him. 'Edouard, my son, why did you run out like a rat in the dark?'

'A holiday,' said Edouard. 'I'm taking a holiday from you. I have taken a room.' I looked at his smiling face, then I broke down completely. I choked with sobs. Then I started talking deliriously.

'There is no reason to take a holiday from me. There is never any reason for anyone to hurt another like this. What are you doing? Why? Why?' I had been mending Edouard's pullover, the green one. It had been worn thin at the collar by the hard beard on his neck. I was proud of that hard beard. I grabbed the scissors and jabbed them into the veins of my left arm. Blood spurted out. It looked ugly. Edouard watched. He didn't rush to stop me. Then he came near and held my hand. 'I'm crazy,' I said. 'I've lost my head,' and with that I flung my head against the wall, violently. I saw some stars, but it wasn't enough to knock me out. I didn't know what I wanted to do. I wanted to damage myself in front of Edouard. I did it again and again. I think I did knock myself out. When I recovered I had a huge bump sticking out of my head. Edouard sat, his arm round me limp without feeling—I remained there for a while and then crumpled. When that was over I got to my feet and went on as if nothing had happened. We laughed and didn't mention his leaving.

'Why did you do this to me, Edouard, is it because I bothered you last night, or this morning?'

'No,' he said, 'I enjoyed it.' A pain took hold of me down between the shoulders. Then it seemed to grip me from one arm across the back and down the other. It was a kind of pain that cried for more pain. Now I wanted to suffer, right there I was already suffering. I handed Edouard a rope I had tied my bags with. Then I tensed myself and waited while I told him to lash me across the back. He lashed me once and then he lashed again.

'Enough,' I screamed. 'I can't stand it, I can't stand it.' But I could. I felt better. 'Hug me, hold me, tighter, tighter, tighter.' Then I came.

I sat on the floor afterwards while we drank a cup of tea. 'I believe you were happy seeing me fall to bits in front of you.'

'Yes,' he said, 'it pleased me.'

'God, how cruel! Go now, and come back soon, I beg you. If not, I will die.' He left and I did die a little, but I hung onto the faint hope that he might come back. Maybe it was only a holiday.

He had told me he had a room. Therefore he had already reserved it while I was cooking for him and sewing the curtains.

I didn't know what to think. I couldn't think about it any more. There was but one thing to do, go out, and get drunk. But I don't drink. So when I'm miserable I go and look for adventure.

Chapter 19

IT WAS TEN O'CLOCK. THE PUBS IN CHELSEA CLOSED AT TEN-THIRTY. I would go straight away. I'd bring home someone, I couldn't be alone.

I dressed quickly, hid my watch in case I fell among thieves, and ran down the street to a Chelsea pub where there was always a crowd of doubtful looking people. I looked; a young man sat at the bar with an empty glass in his hand. I would offer him a drink. I don't know how these things are done in England, as I never go to pubs, but I find that whatever you do in life you fool no one. Going straight up to him, I said, 'Quick, let me fill up that glass before the place closes.' I didn't even wait to hear how he sounded, or find out whether he was working or loafing. I didn't care. I was after a thrill and here it was. He was well over six feet tall, with immense shoulders.

On top of his sturdy neck was a small head with straight fair hair. The features were sharp and neat, the eyes blue. He had no expression on his face. 'Hello, closing time!' I exclaimed. 'What are you up to? I'm going home—want some dinner?' Ten minutes later we were home and ten minutes after that I had tried everything to seduce him and failed. Now how to get rid of the man.

He picked at and left his food, my good food. He was impossible to communicate with and he would have nothing to do with me. I went to the little room to prepare coffee, and when I returned, he was in the cupboard, touching and trying on my clothes. 'What on earth are you doing in there?'

He gave a start, 'I was only looking at that suede jacket of yours,' he said. 'I want to try it '

'Put it down, you can't do that in other people's homes. Besides it isn't mine.'

'I only want to try it on,' he said.

'It belongs to my friend!'

'He won't mind,' he said, continuing to touch the coat.

'Yes he will,' I said. 'You're sweating and smelly in the armpits. Smell stays. I don't want my friend to make a row. Sit down. If you want to do something, take off that fine sweater you're wearing and let me stop the run. You're lucky, chum,' I went on. 'Just in time!' I steam-rollered him into taking it off and went into raves about it. 'What a lovely article. I am in the business. I mean, my father was in materials. This is such excellent quality—did you pay a lot for it?'

'It was a present,' he said.

'Someone who had a very high opinion of you, that's for sure. In whose flat had he helped himself to that?

The moment he did take it off, I forgot how imperative it was to get rid of him. He was magnificent. The only way to get him out without a scandal and without my jacket was if someone miraculously arrived and stayed until he left. If only I could telephone someone, anything not to be alone with this man. As I sewed the sweater, I asked him about himself and told him about myself—how I might suddenly be on the brink of becoming rich, and how, if all went well, I would go and live in a better place. 'If only my business deal comes off you could come and stay,' I said. 'Big strong man like you could be useful. Are you working now?'

'No,' he said.

'Would you like to make some money modelling? All you have to do is stand there. They pay five pounds an hour—one hour's work a day. That's all! Look—take the telephone, dial the number yourself, I'll see if I can find my agent friend.' I got him to ring me a whole series of numbers. Nemone would come but they weren't in. Ricki was out, Ronnie wasn't there. 'I'm going to lose my jacket,' I thought. Aloud I continued, 'More to be done. Look, another run.' And skipping from one subject to another, 'Ah, I have an idea. I know a French girl who models, she could give you all the dope—ring her.'

I gave the number of Edouard's bar and he dialled it. I asked for Edouard in French; he came to the telephone. It must have been midnight. 'Edouard,' I said, 'trust me. I am in trouble. There's a man here. He is immense. I can't fight him, nor can you, but come anyway and quick, quick, or I'll lose my suede jacket.'

'Je viens,' he said. The next twenty minutes passed like twenty days. I sat there pulling out threads with my teeth and sticking the needle into my fingers. I was excited at the thought of seeing Edouard back. Then I was scared. Suppose I got him into a fight. This man would kill Edouard. Edouard was strong and beautiful, but this was a giant. He started fidgeting. He was getting bored.

'That'll be enough now,' he said. 'I must be going.'

'But that girl we rang might come and we could have a grand time. What do you say?' All this while I was fiddling round and spitting out threads, like Penelope waiting for Ulysses. That's right—I was Penelope. Edouard with his hirsute head was Ulysses, and the giant without his shirt was Hercules. Hercules! Ulysses! and Penelope! If only Edouard would come. I couldn't keep it up much longer. If Edouard doesn't come I'll lose my jacket.

Then we heard noises in the passage outside. It sounded like more than one person. The squeak of the rubbers was Edouard. I heard the dit, dit, dit of high heels. Had she materialised, this woman I had just invented to keep Hercules with me? I sighed with relief as a key slipped into the door and I heard voices. Edouard dashed into the room on guard. Behind him, looking somewhat swollen, was a big female. Edouard looked at the man sitting in his singlet and said to me in French, 'You could have chosen someone my size. I introduced him and then Edouard introduced the girl. They spoke French and I asked them to continue doing so. This way all communication would be impossible and the man would leave.

I broke the silence with a jolly, 'I've done it! It's ready now!' and handed him back his garment. I helped him on with it and said under my breath, 'I'm afraid there is going to be a bit of trouble and it looks as if I might even join you. It isn't really my house here either.' So he left. No sooner had he closed the door than I threw my arms around Edouard and kissed him. Then I did the same to the girl which she accepted shyly. I studied her for a minute. She wasn't pretty, she had a fleshy nose and a broad face. She might have been a Slav peasant except for her 'indoor' skin. She had the sick look of the women who only go out of the house at night. She was young and buxom, without the healthy connotation of that word. I couldn't think what Edouard saw in her. She had a pleasant smile and her teeth were small and good. She looked clean, but she had a fat putty look about her. Her lids were heavily blacked and she wore no other make-up. She looked weird.

'This is Lily,' Edouard said.

'Are you French?' I asked.

'Yes.'

'Are you studying here like Edouard?'

'Yes.' Then she asked for the bathroom and went there.

'C'est une putain,' Edouard whispered in my ear. 'She's a prostitute, I met her an hour ago at the club. She asked me over and I dated her. I'm going home with her.'

'Stay here with me,' I begged. 'Please stay, both of you.'

A month before, I had had a funny dream. I had not wanted to sleep with any woman, but a strange situation kept coming to my mind repeatedly and I mentioned it to Edouard. I knew he and his friend Lucien often had a girl together. I imagined a situation in which Edouard and Lucien brought a girl home to me. Fooling around they got hold of me by force and obliged me to go down on her.

My mind flew back to that dream. Why don't these two stay with me?

I suggested it but he didn't seem very keen. Nor did she. What else could I do? They left after he promised to telephone me the next day. I couldn't stand being without news of him for more than a day and I found him the following afternoon at the bar. He told me he was now living with her and that she was a real prostitute. There was another girl there, also a prostitute, and they liked him.

'What about the room you took?'

'Oh,' he said, 'I like to have a place of my own.'

'Where is it?' I asked.

'On top of the Golden Egg in Charing Cross Road,' he told me.

'And how can I get in touch with you? At Lily's?'
'I won't give you Lily's address.'
'Why not? Why exclude me?'
'You can ring me at the bar '

Chapter 20

THE NEXT DAY HE CAME TO LUNCH, BUT IT WASN'T A HAPPY LUNCH. Something was different. He had only been gone for two days, but it was no longer the same. I tried to get near him but he wouldn't have me.

'Be kind to me, Edouard, please.' He eventually let me near. I laid my head on his shoulder and then I smelled a new smell. Something was indeed different. 'Edouard, you don't smell the same. What's happened?'

'Tu m'ennuies,' he said. 'You bore me.'

He left without glancing back. Usually he turned and looked. That was his sign of affection, but he just walked away now that I was in need of that extra bit of kindness. I must leave the country. I would go to Paris. This was no life for me. I telephoned Ricki and told her I was leaving.

'Do you mean to say you haven't enough here with us, with Nemone, with your other friends, with Jimmie's screen play you promised to help with. You mean you're going to rat on us all because of this creature. You've scraped the floors and I've lent you furniture, you have an ice box and a phone—stay! Give it a chance. And he did come to your rescue over that giant.'

When I phoned Nemone, she said, 'Your frog is far nicer than my grot bag.'

'Your what?' I asked, suddenly thinking she had some medical problem.

'My grot bag, my husband, my grotty husband. I tell you he's far worse than Edouard. As he was leaving the house this morning I slipped and cut my finger on a meat knife. Blood spurted out and

I called to him to get me some alcohol and plaster. It was a deep cut and a messy one. Do you know what he did? He saw me holding my hand, fell onto the stairs outside the kitchen and said, "God, how awful, get me a glass of water. The sight of blood makes me sick". So we all put up with things.'

Meantime, I was trying to overcome my depression yet refused every opportunity to do so. All I wanted was to wait for the next time Edouard came. I hoped he would come to me daily at least for lunch, but even that was not happening. When he did come I had a long talk with him.

'Edouard, be my friend. I am terribly unhappy. Shall I go to Paris and forget?'

'Je te veux ici,' he said, pointing to the floor. He wanted me in London. I was grateful for these words, words that meant nothing, that demanded no proof or sacrifice from him. Yet they decided me to stay.

'Look after me when I beg you. I am sick, sick, sick. It was rotten of you to make me think you were coming when you had taken a room elsewhere. Make it up to me now. Be kind to me.

'I've heard all that before,' said Edouard impatiently.

'You swine!' I screamed. I turned on him like a wild beast. 'I'll ruin you, I'll poison you, I'll see you're kicked out of this country. How dare you say that after what I've done for you?'

'I must phone Lily,' he said taking no notice. He dialled the number which I memorised as I watched him, but he dialled it wrong.

'I thought I had it,' he said, 'I must have it somewhere.'

'If you have the number of the street I can find it for you, Edouard.' With that I dialled Directory Enquiry and while I spoke to the operator I asked him for the number of the street where she lived. Unguardedly he told me and I told him to write down the number the operator gave me. He telephoned Lily and they spoke for twenty minutes. She wanted to know whether she should change her room now that she was sharing with him. He said he would discuss that with her later.

I was irritated with the conversation. If he lived with her and slept with her, why the hell couldn't he stay with me for the few minutes we had together instead of jabbering to her.

'Tell me about your life with Lily,' I said after a long silence. 'I know nothing of what you're doing. You are so far from me now. Do you make love to her all the time?'

'Only when she wants. She has men all day, so she isn't often in the mood.'

'Is she affectionate, do you kiss her?'

'Kiss her!' he said horrified. 'Are you mad? Kiss a putain!' He made the word sound dirty.

'So you just make love to her when you feel like it? And when she does, do you then refuse?'

'Get on with your cooking,' he said, then continued: 'I'd like to help her open an account or something. She wastes money.'

'Edouard, you are a fool. A whore's a whore. They don't want you to open accounts so that they can save money. They want to be beaten, to be told to get onto the streets again and bring back more dough. Otherwise, with two clients, they can pay for their room and board. This is a business, dear boy! They have to be kicked back when they're dead tired. That's their profession. Open an account for her! Grow up. If you want to live off a whore, do it right instead of taking the risk of being known as a ponce and being thrown out of the country.'

Chapter 21

TWO DAYS LATER, EDOUARD CAME ROUND. AGAIN, I ASKED HIM WHERE he was living and he didn't answer. He didn't know I had found the telephone number through the address he had given me. I asked him how much money he now had in his account. There had been one hundred and twenty pounds when we parted.

'A hundred and forty pounds,' he said. 'Not only have I not opened an account for her, but I make her put money into mine, and I boxed her ear the other night. I told her I wanted thirty pounds more by the end of the week.' It was so hateful. The boy I loved, living off a prostitute nineteen years old, and me, telling him how to get money from her. Did I want to be part of Edouard's life at this price? Was this what I did not want him to exclude me from? I must go see her, spy on her. I had to know. I refused to be ignored. I had everything on my side—time, money, and I was in my own country. I'd win in the end. Of course I would.

I would have them watched, get a detective, wait for her at the bar and follow them home. As he left I went towards him. Just to touch him, a friendly contact. I lifted my arms, he pushed me brusquely away. I grabbed hold of his sleeve and pulled him to me. I didn't care if he lashed out, I was angry, humiliated. He tore himself free and walked away.

I sat down and wrote to his father. 'Mr. Solda: Edouard has been my guest for the last four months. I have introduced him everywhere, given him clothes and money, found him a school—and where is he now? Living with a nineteen-year-old prostitute. He has become a cheap ponce at twenty-one.' I tore it up and started again. 'I asked Edouard if he wanted to share a flat with me and he said he did. So I took an expensive flat for which, needless to say, I would not dream of making him pay.' That was awful, just awful. Again: 'Sir: In the interest of your family's good name I suggest'—that was hardly better. I wrote one letter after another—the schoolmaster, the abandoned lover, the disappointed god-father. They all stank, I stank. Why was I bringing his father into it? If Edouard wouldn't help me, I'd get help from his own family. I'd do anything, ruin him. The one I finally sent off was a little better. 'Dear Mr. Solda: I feel it is my duty to inform you that I will take no further responsibility for your son. He is not living with us.' (Us being Ronnie and Rachel, the happy middle-aged couple he had so sweetly imagined them to be.) 'He has not registered with the authorities, he has not thanked the people where he was a guest for four months and he hardly goes to classes. If there is anything you can do to bring him to his senses, let me know. I have given up. I do not even know where he is nor with whom he is living.' It was a stupid letter but I sent it. If he didn't want me as a friend, he would have me as an enemy. But I would be with him. I'd rather he hated me than lose contact with him. I would make trouble for him, I could and I would.

I don't know how I managed to get to sleep that night but I eventually did. Then the telephone rang. It was Edouard, saying, 'I ventured to know how you were.' It sounded funny—and Edouard was never contrite. I was half asleep. He spoke amiably, but I was suspicious. Perhaps he needed me as I had needed him when that big giant came, but the conversation went no further. He rang off.

The following evening Lily rang me at one-thirty in the morning. 'You're the only friend of Edouard's I know—I'm sorry to trouble you.' She was in tears. 'What shall I do? We came home together an hour ago, then he went out to get milk and he hasn't returned. I am so worried.'

'It can only be one of two things,' I said. 'Either he has been arrested by the police, in which case all will be well provided he gives a proper address and doesn't say he is living with you. The other possibility? I don't know. I hope he hasn't been killed, he's far too beautiful to die. Maybe he's been kidnapped. Don't worry, it's probably nothing. Tell him to ring me when he comes in.

He'll be back, and if he isn't, he'll call back tomorrow, but he'll be back,' I said, wishing I were talking about him and me. Half an hour later Edouard called. He had returned. They had been filming in the street and he had been carried away by the excitement of the shooting.

The next day I decided to find out more about the two. I would go to her apartment. I got there at the hour Edouard was at school. She lived off Paddington. All the houses in the road let rooms. Hers was a rather prosperous, creamy colour that is used in London. It always struck me as extraordinary that, in a dirty town like London, people painted their houses in light colours. I looked down the list of names and rang when I came to hers—'Miss Lily.' There was no answer. I went to a flower shop and bought a small plant in a pot.

I was ashamed—I was being false. They wrapped the pot up in cellophane and I walked back to Lily's. I rang the housekeeper's bell and she came to the door.

'I'm looking for Miss Lily,' I said.

'Is she expecting you?'

'Of course.'

'Well, it's up on the third floor, No. 7, or let me see. Hasn't she changed rooms?'

'Oh, don't worry, dear, if she's not in one she'll be in the other. I'll find her.'

Perhaps I'd find Edouard sleeping there. Who knows? He might have overslept. But that wasn't my purpose, I didn't want to see Edouard—I wanted rather to find out about him, go through his private papers, see what was new. I opened the door of a room and it was empty. I went to the first room the housekeeper had indicated and knocked on it.

'Who is it?' answered Lily.

'It is I, Edouard's friend.' She said she was coming to open the door which she did. She might have been suspicious but she smiled at me, then turned away and got back into bed. I stared. The creature who had opened the door was nothing to do with the overgrown student I had seen a week ago. What I saw here before me was an animal, a big, voluptuous lioness. A thick flamboyant mass of chestnut hair fell over her face, down her shoulders to her back like lava. When she had come to the flat she had it drawn back from her forehead—it had looked flat and straight. Now it came to life. Everything about her came to life. She unfurled before me like a flag. She wore a printed black, transparent flowered nightdress which showed her body through it. She had glorious shoulders, and a mass of rich, young, womanly flesh. She tapered slowly down to long slim legs and long slim hands—slim except for a slight fatty quality through the palms that made them look nearly indecent. She walked back to her bed barefoot and got in, drawing the sheets up to her waist. She wasn't the same girl—this was something else, huge, bag, juicy fuck. Now I saw why Edouard was there.

The blinds were drawn and the gas fire was on. England, with its gas fires permanently on, bringing some semblance of warmth to a house without heat. She smiled as she took the pot from me.

'J'aime les plantes,' she said. There were two beds in the room and I recognised Edouard's things. The floor, the tables, the desk, everything was a mess. Papers, cigarettes, contraceptives, scent, everything that should be lying about in a whore's bedroom. 'I'm glad you came. Sit down,' she said. 'I am not busy today.'

I sat on the end of the bed and started tidying the things round me as I spoke. 'Look at Edouard's wind jacket,' I said. 'What a state it's in. And here, these trousers of his. I'll have to wash them,' I said, emptying them out and putting what was in them on the table

'I take his things to the cleaners,' she said. 'They give them back in a short time.'

'Why waste the money?' I asked. 'I have always washed them, I will take them.' She did not object. She was genuinely pleased to see me. I could see she trusted me and was glad I had come, and it made me uncomfortable—I would have preferred to be treated as the spy I was.

His leather despatch case lay on the floor. It was full. I had given it to him and he had written his name on it in ink that wouldn't rub off. A cheap plastic one would have been as useful. That was all he wanted from it—usefulness. While we talked I turned the thing upside down on the bed in front of us both as if it was my right.

'Oh, the shit!' I cried in fun. 'He stole my eyedrops.' I picked up the bottle.

'Yes,' she said, 'he has an eye that is inflamed. Take it back.' I put it in my pocket and looked through the rest of his things. One thing only interested me—his bank book.

'You were sweet the other night when I was worried about him disappearing — thank you,' she said.

'Lily, I understand he did to you what he once did to me, only I hope it was less painful.'

'What do you mean?' she replied, not understanding.

'When he slapped you across the face,' I said. 'When he did it to me, I thought I had gone deaf.'

'What is this nonsense? Edouard has never laid a finger on me. I wouldn't allow it. What made him say a thing like that?'

'Maybe to feel important. Maybe each person in life plays a role according to the way he wants to appear. Maybe we should deal with people as they are to us and not on the basis of what we find out about them from others. Who knows why he told me he hit you!'

She was upset. Then I found his bank book. I looked at his balance. One hundred and twenty pounds. The liar! Dirty little liar playing the tough man, pretending to beat the tart and take her money. So you will have a hundred and forty pounds in the bank, will you? I was livid. Again I was on the outside, he was trusting her and not me. How could he leave his bank book around. 'Tell no one how much money you have,' I had warned him. And here it was, the bank book in front of her, in front of me. Flabby, juvenile, adolescent. You beat whores, push them around, make them give you money. Why wasn't the balance a hundred and forty or fifty or two hundred by now? Yet I was glad the sum was still the same. He wasn't a ponce, he was just a kid trying something new.

'You know what I do?' she asked.

'Well, as you're always at home, I guessed. I hope he doesn't go round telling everybody, you could be thrown out of the country and he could be sent to prison. It's a terribly serious offence.'

'I know. I will have to leave this place.'

I was suddenly tired. 'Lily, I must go, I've talked too much. I'll take these things and wash them. Tell Edouard to come to lunch tomorrow and get them.'

'And I must get up and see my priest; he said he'd help me.'

I heard her say something about a priest, but I wasn't really interested in her problems right then—I was interested in my own. I went to kiss her good-bye. She was gentle, trusting.

'Merci pour la plante. I must go and put a candle to St. Anthony,' she said.

'What have you lost?'

'An expensive cigarette lighter. I know who took it—it's a client of mine. It's hardly worth making a few pounds to lose twice the amount in a lighter. He'll come back—he says he loves me! But I shall be moving and I shan't leave my address with anybody.'

My heart dropped—she was moving! How would I find her then?

Chapter 22

I MADE MY WAY SLOWLY HOME. I PUT THE THINGS I HAD BROUGHT TO wash, on the bed. I laid my head on them and fell asleep, a painful, restless, tormented hour. I felt twice as tired when I awoke. Where was I going? What should I do? I would talk it over with him tomorrow at lunch. Then I got up and washed his things and put them over the fire to dry while I sat watching.

Next day, at one o'clock when he still hadn't appeared, I rang Lily. The housekeeper answered. 'Miss Lily has gone. She has left no address.' I asked if I could write and she said she didn't know if Miss Lily would return for the letters. I went mad. She's gone. He's gone. He's left me. He's cut me out. I don't even know where he is. He didn't come to lunch. He won't get away with it. I'll fix him. I'll cause trouble for him. See what I'll do! I telephoned the bar.

'When Edouard comes tell him to phone me urgently. It is to do with his residence in this country.' If it's war, it's war. I'll fight to win. They told me he wasn't expected until seven that evening, but that under the circumstances they wondered if it was safe to let him work. 'If I can get to him first I can let you know if it will be alright or not. In any case, wait till I find out.'

At six o'clock Edouard telephoned. 'What's all this about?' he asked.

'We can talk about that later. Weren't you supposed to come to lunch?'

'I had to move apartments with Lily.'

'Nothing stopped you telephoning, did it, Edouard?'

'Well, what's this about the bar. They said you rang that there might be trouble!'

'There certainly might be if you don't watch yourself. Today you might not be taken on at the bar, tomorrow you might not be taken on anywhere, and the day after you might get kicked out of the country.'

'Ha,' he grunted, 'Je viens.' He came round immediately.

'Edouard, I will not put up with any more from you. You were expected to lunch today. If you don't come for some reason, then you must phone and tell me. Take some trouble over me; I have taken enough over you. Whatever I can do for you, I can do twice as much against you. If fact, I have already written to your father about you. The next thing I shall do is to start writing some other letters to some other people and then my boy—this!' I banged my left fist into my open right palm, just like he had done to me when Rachel said he could stay on at the house. 'Where are you staying now?'

'I'll never tell you,' he said, 'and you'll never find out.'

'If that's how you feel, maybe you won't work at the bar anymore either and maybe I'll find out anyway. I can, you know. I have lots and lots of resources, Edouard, and nothing better to do than to get even with you.'

He left externally indifferent, but he was scared. At seven o'clock he telephoned me. 'I am at the bar. They won't take me on till they have spoken to you. What do you want from me?'

'I don't want to suffer any more because of you, that's all I want. I will telephone them and see if they will take you back, but I am warning you—no, I'm threatening you.'

Changing the subject, he said, 'Michel is arriving tomorrow. Do you want to come to the station with me?' I couldn't answer him. What should I answer? I was 'the Queer' in his letter to Michel; now he was taking me to meet him. I did not know where I stood.

Chapter 23

EDOUARD MET ME AT WESTMINSTER ABBEY. THE SUN WAS SHINING and we talked on a bench in the park. I watched him as he looked into the hard light of the sun, the pupils of his eyes getting smaller as he screwed up his face to avoid the glare. His hair was still long and untidy, he held a cigarette in between his teeth.

'Come just once and spend the night at my place, won't you?'

'I can't,' he answered. I stood up to go to the train.

'Your eye is bloodshot,' I said.

'I know.'

Michel was not surprised to see me there with Edouard. What then had Edouard written about me?

Michel had written no more to the house. Nor had he answered my letter to him saying that I would help him if Edouard didn't. Edouard must have told him to write to the bar. I would go to the Post Office one day and tell them Edouard's letters were to be forwarded to my place. I would brandish his passport and thus be able to go on reading his mail. It never struck me what it must have been like for him, living in a house where he was not even sure of receiving his mail and even then only after it had been read by me. It seemed that since he was not frank with me I had every right to spy on him. I must have been lost in thought when I heard them shouting my name. They were already in a cab and I got in with them.

'Go to Soho,' Edouard told the driver. I pointed out Buckingham Palace and the Mall to Michel, but like Edouard he was not interested. I felt he was only waiting for me to leave so he could talk to his friend. As we approached Shaftesbury Avenue, Edouard told the driver to stop the cab. He turned to me and looking icily said, 'Tu peux descendre ici'—you can get out here.'

I got out crushed and humiliated and wandered aimlessly through Berwick Market. The sun went down and everything went cold. All next day I waited for Edouard's call but it never came. I lay about, alternately smouldering with anger and meditating revenge, or bitterly sorry for myself. The following day he rang. I didn't give him time to speak. I cursed him, called him a swine, said I'd get him, he'd pay for it and in the middle of the tirade I hung up. I went over what I had said to him.

'It costs threepence in a new telephone box and fourpence in an old one. Can't you spare that for a friend? I'll ruin you. I'll see you can't go anywhere!' What had all that meant? I didn't know, but in the back of my mind, I was going to have him expelled from every country in the world. I would denounce him as a ponce. I'd see that the police knew he was living off the earnings of a whore. They were hot on that! The French police would want to know about that. All the police in the world would be after him—he would be doomed, damned, destroyed.

But I didn't know where he lived. How could I prove he was living with a prostitute? And she—what would happen to her? She had been so sweet to me. I had already played a dirty trick arriving with those Judas flowers. She had hidden nothing from me, neither what she did nor how she lived. It would mean denouncing her too. That would be terrible. Years ago, a man I knew went insane over a young actor. The man was a sharp, pitiless lawyer, and the boy a Spaniard . . . delightful, friendly, innocent. The lawyer had promised him help in his film career. He had taken him to America, literally sequestered him and made his life intolerable. When they returned to Europe the boy packed, tried to leave, but found the man had locked the hotel room door. The boy went out of the window, found a room and started to earn his living again. Within two days, the man had put the police onto him. He accused him of having stolen money, jewels and shares, of being a Communist and organising orgies. The charges were so absurd that the police understood immediately that the boy was innocent. Nevertheless, the lawyer had informed the U.S. Embassy, the Spanish Consulate and the Italian police and the boy finally had to leave Rome. The basest, vilest thing I had ever come across. Here I was doing exactly the same thing.

Unable to bear my own evil thoughts, I rang Rachel. 'Promise me you'll never inform any authority over Edouard,' she said. 'You brought him here as your friend and it's on a friendship basis you have to solve your problems with him. Next thing the authorities will be asking where he lives, who you are, who Ricki is, who Jimmie is, who everyone is. Never, never, do such a thing.' I promised I wouldn't.

I hardly slept that night. Lately I had been sleeping passably well, but in the morning I would wake up anguished after nightmares. I would be in some situation where I was getting my own back on Edouard—I'd have him beaten up, drugged, denounced, shamed. I thought of all I could do to harm him, but I could never find the right means to use against him, everything failed. My forehead seemed taut like a drum, my back ached, my neck was stiff, I wasn't eating, I was breaking up.

Ricki begged me to accept defeat. 'Let go,' she begged. 'Let go.'

'I have wept like a fool for hours every morning. I can't go on, I haven't eaten, I have lost twenty pounds.'

'Which of us has not wept?' Ricki answered. 'You must get hold of yourself, find something to do, get a job, work on Jimmie's script . . . We have all cried, I cried for years . . . and I couldn't run away. I had children, duties and a home. You can still escape.' She had spoken with suppressed anguish. So others have also wept—I had forgotten that . . . my own pain was enveloping me. My Brazilian friend said, 'Leave, go to Rome. Forget. It will pass . . . you don't have to fight.'

I went so far as ringing Paris. Mirella sympathised, 'It takes a year or so. I am sorry. Come over to Paris. We still love you.'

Murray said less, but he understood. 'Poor old thing—first time for you—that's bad. Remember when I went through it?' I did remember. We used to telephone each other talking sometimes for an hour or more in the evenings, thrashing it out. 'You'd better come over to Paris,' he said. 'You have your friends and your car. You'll be freer . . . come on.' It was tempting. If they had suggested it before, it would have been alright. Now I wanted revenge. I wouldn't leave this way. This was a defeat. I had asked so little, so very little . . .

The next day Michel rang. 'Could he and Edouard come for lunch.' They arrived an hour later with Lily. I hardly had a moment alone with Edouard, but while the other two were eating, I got him to myself in the bathroom.

'Come and stay this evening. I beg you.'

'Non,' he said.

'Then come and spend an hour with me after work at midnight, please!'

'I'll see,' he said.

That evening I was expecting Ricki, Ronnie, Rachel, my Brazilian friend and Jimmie, the young writer, a wonderful looking young man who had written a best seller. I had difficulty with the meal. My stove had but one grill and my ambitions were great. The things wouldn't cook, the hotplate wasn't hot enough, everything that could went wrong. I should have been harrassed, but I wasn't. They would understand and Edouard was coming . . . so what did anything matter?

That evening all my friends sat around, giving me advice. It was so strange, a grown-up like myself sitting there, saucepan in hand, while my young and successful friends advised me how to contend with my non-lover.

Jimmie said, 'Is this the creature that you want to share your life with—give up everything for? It's not possible.'

'Come with me when I go to America!' the Brazilian repeated.

'A trip to Rome always fixes things,' Rachel said. 'He'll come back . . . one day.'

'Edouard will be coming,' I told them, and to prove it—I cannot think why I wanted to prove it—I rang him up at the bar.

'I'm counting on you to come,' I said. 'Don't let me down.'

'I'm not coming,' he said. I hung up instinctively . . . to prevent my friends in the room from knowing. But of course I told them a moment later. So he had now humiliated me in front of them. Now he had to come, he had to. I'd make him. I picked up the receiver and dialled again.

'Edouard,' I said. 'Please yourself . . . But if you don't come this evening, I shall denounce you. I'll see that you get thrown out of England tomorrow.' Again I hung up. 'That was a terrible thing to do!' I said looking round, angry, ashamed and yet pleased.

Jimmie answered, 'It shows something constructive, evil or not. Do you good, kicking him around like that. Scare him a bit, you'll get results.' Ricki just put her hand on mine. Her eyes were full of tears.

Rachel said, 'You're in a dangerous mood. Don't denounce him. You would hate yourself . . . and the authorities would ask you what you were doing with him. Before you knew where you were we would all be involved.' I was almost certain Edouard would come while my friends were still there. It was the least he could do. I had lied to everyone for him, told them I was a dotty old thing with a passion for the French boy . . . that it was enough he should be near me occasionally. I hadn't told a soul that we had been lovers, but he had pushed me around. Why shouldn't he be embarrassed for a change. I recalled the day I went to see him at work. He told me to keep away from the bar. 'If you have a friend you're ashamed of, give him up, don't use him,' I had replied. I returned home dejected and miserable. Then I remember putting on a record called 'Desafinado'. I played if often but till then the name meant nothing to me. 'Desafinado' in Brazilian means 'ill fitting—ill tuned, what does not go together'. . . an old woman and a young man or an old man and a young man—a young man who likes girls. Edouard arrived just as they were leaving. His hair was still uncut and fell over his face. He wore his old worn wind jacket. I looked at him and compared him to Jimmie and the Brazilian; Jimmie was clean and handsome, the Brazilian looked like the lithograph of an elegant supple Japanese horse with a black splodge of a mane. Both men were handsome. They had style, charm and friendship for me. Edouard's face was sullen, sombre . . . a face without light. Yet, damn him, his was the face I wanted.

I did everything I could to make him stay the night. Once again he left me empty . . . But at least I had seen him. I wouldn't leave our next meeting to chance. I asked him to lunch next day. He wouldn't accept. I told him he had to, I made him promise he'd come. First he had said he would live with me. That's why I remained in London. Even after he had left me, he insisted I stay in London. Couldn't he at least have put his arms round me, told me not to worry, that he would come. Anything to make up for the misery he had caused.

The next day at four in the afternoon Lily rang.

'I'm waiting for Edouard to come to lunch,' I said.

'I've spoken with him,' she said. 'He told me to tell you he slept late and won't have time to come.'

'I will kill him,' I said.

'Edouard says you are capable of anything.'

'That's in theory; you'll see how it works in practice.'

'Why do you want to hurt him?' she asked. 'Hurting him is hurting me.'

'I don't want to hurt you. I think you're a marvellous girl . . . but you mean nothing to me. I want to get even with him.'

'What are you going to do to him?'

'Get him thrown out of the country.'

'I know you can do that,' she said. 'Where will it get you? You still won't have him.'

'It will do him good, Lily. He has to learn a lesson. He's put me through too much.' I told her how I had made a new life for him and how he now excluded me from everything. 'I've done everything for him and still he doesn't trust me.'

'I do,' she said.

'He won't tell me where you two are living.'

'I will,' she said. 'I'll give you the number straight away. Come over immediately.' I wrote down her address and telephone number. 'Please don't tell Edouard . . . you know . . . it will cause trouble between us. He may want to protect me from you . . . but I know I don't need protection. I will wait for you on the street, my bell is out of order.'

She was standing outside when I arrived. She greeted me without emotion. She seemed detached . . . and as I got to know her better I saw she always acted as if she were suppressing her feelings, her face almost expressionless. I could never get used to it. But I knew she felt things deeply.

I was holding a small parcel carefully under my arm. 'Is that for me,' she asked.

'For both of us,' I said as I opened it on the table. I had thought it would be nice to bring some home-cooked food. I had prepared a borscht and there was a small carton of cream and a huge veal cutlet.

'Borscht,' she cried. 'I was brought up on it. My family was Polish.'

We ate and the borscht did to us what drink does to others. It put us on the same wavelength. We relaxed. 'It's a nice flat,' I said.

'Yes, thanks to my priest. He lent me the money. I'll have to pay him back.'

Every priest has his prostitute and every prostitute her priest. I wondered if she had a great cross hanging on the wall as well. 'Are you Catholic,' I asked.

'I'm Jewish,' she said.

A Jewish nineteen-year-old French-Polish prostitute working in London. 'I'm Jewish.' She could be my daughter. I felt an extra tenderness for her.

'What are we going to tell Edouard about your being here?' she asked. 'He'll want to know how you found the apartment.'

'Tell him that you had a telephone conversation with me and in the middle of it I asked you to hold on a minute. In the meantime, I had the call traced.'

'Don't let me down,' she said. 'I don't want to lose Edouard. I love him.'

'I'll never let you down, Lily. But I might do anything to him.'

'Jo, listen to me, please. I want to tell you a story. It's about a girl called Danielle, a friend of mine. A few months ago I was living with her in a block of flats. We . . . were . . . both doing the same thing. One day she got to talking with this priest. He was Italian and so was Danielle's mother so I guess she thought they had something in common. They became friendly. He told her he was a priest and asked her to translate a tract into French for him. She accepted . . . it seemed harmless at the time. Well, you know how it goes . . . he had to be around a lot to watch if she was doing it properly and . . . after a while fell in love with her. At the time she had an Armenian lover who wanted to marry her. He had offered her money and a home and told her to stop . . . working. He was very jealous and possessive. Danielle wasn't interested in him. Being a prostitute is a very special existence . . . we like the adventure and the independence and Danielle didn't want to be tied down. They had some terrible scenes. The Armenian said he couldn't live without her. But he couldn't make her change her mind. So he telephoned the police and denounced her for prostitution . . . The priest couldn't do a thing to help and she was made to leave the country.'

Lily looked at me to see if I understood. I felt sick. What is the matter with someone who won't take no for an answer. I wanted Edouard . . . and tried to force him to play the game my way . . . and he wouldn't. But my case was different, wasn't it? I didn't want to own Edouard. I didn't even force my attentions on him when we were together. I just wanted to be part of his life, even help paint the house he'd choose when he got married. But I was helpless against the cruel games he had played with my heart. I had lost him and still I loved him. All I asked from him now was a month . . . of kindness and consideration and not to be excluded. Later perhaps I would heal. He owed it to me after the little, the very little I had asked of him.

'Don't think about denouncing Edouard,' Lily said. 'Nothing can cure the pain. Hurting him won't make you feel better.'

'You don't know how he has deceived and tormented me, Lily. You couldn't. I can't just let it end this way . . . I feel empty, destroyed. I just want a little in return from him now . . . But that little I want.'

'What do you want,' she asked.

'To see him. That he should ring every day. My whole purpose of being in England no longer exists without him. I shall be gone within a month. I have lost him I know . . . Let me lose him as painlessly as possible. All I ask is that we should not part in anger . . . that I see him daily so I can feel all this has not been wasted. And we remain in contact.'

'Nothing is wasted,' she said. 'You have learned something. I have learned something, he has learned something. And if all you want is to see him, I will try to arrange it.'

'I can't hurt you, Lily. You trusted me.'

'But you will if you hurt him.'

'Then see that he doesn't provoke me . . . How is he by the way?'

'Not well,' she said. 'He told me you wished him to go to the hospital for his eyes. He went with me yesterday. They gave him some medicine.'

'What's wrong, do you know?'

'They didn't tell us.'

'Lily, he should come to the hospital with me, not with you. I am his mother so to speak. I can take care of him, and I'm worried, about his eye.'

'He doesn't complain, but I don't think he's well.'

'Shall we ring him?' I asked.

'I'll ring him and then you talk.' She rang him at the bar and said I wanted to speak to him.

'I'm at Lily's flat, Edouard. I found your address by tracing a telephone call. I'm sick of you, sick of everything. I'm going . . . going to leave England. I want you to come over and talk with me,' I said gravely.

'I've asked one of the boys, Alain, to take over for me but he can't. I won't be able to get away.'

I didn't know whether or not he was telling the truth. I didn't insist. 'Perhaps you can have lunch with me tomorrow?' He said he couldn't. 'We shall see what we shall see,' I said quietly and hung up. Lily had said nothing, and when I was finished she changed the subject.

'Look,' she said. 'Here is a letter from the first man who seduced me. He still sends me money after five years.' She went to her drawer. I recognised pictures of Edouard lying at the bottom. 'Those pictures of Edouard?'

'He gave them to me.'

'I took them.' There was one of Edouard in Paris, wearing a cowboy hat holding Mirella's daughter in his arms. Another sitting outside her house with a guitar on his knee. I had forgotten them. There were the others—the one taken at Orly when we went to pick up that model, who warned me against Edouard. Others on a picnic and one in Whitehall, holding a horse by his reins while an enormous Grenadier Guard sat impassive, in his red and gold uniform.

'He was supposed to send these to his father,' I said. 'That's why I took them.' As I came to the end, she handed me a letter from Lyon.

'Five years,' she said, 'for five years he's been sending me money and thinking of me. That's why I say when you love I believe it's forever.'

'You were fourteen at the time?'

'Nearly fifteen. I'll tell you how we met. I remember it clearly, as if it were today. We were living at Lyon at the time. It was a summer afternoon and school was over. I was crossing a bridge, trying to catch up with a girl called Arlette. Arlette was a year older than me and the prettiest girl in the school. She was capricious and spoilt but she had long, curly, beautifully golden hair. I must have been ten yards behind her when I saw a middle-aged man take off his hat and bow to her. He said, "Mademoiselle, may I introduce myself. I saw you running along the bridge and thought you looked so pretty, permit me to . . ." Arlette burst out laughing right in his face."Mais, Monsieur," she said, "regardez votre calvitie!" —look at your bald head. I can't forget the face of that poor man. Arlette tripped away merrily, and the man just stood, crushed in the middle of the street. I went up to him and said, "Oh, Monsieur, don't take any notice of Arlette. She's spoilt because she's pretty, everyone in the school says so." Ten minutes later I was in his car and he was driving me round the outskirts of Lyon and into the country. I was left free at home. My mother never asked me where I went. She was often out and I never even had to lie to her. The man was sweet to me. He fondled me a little. I remember he had a light grey mohair suit on and I admired the material. He was pleased and said it came from England. When he took me back, he said he wanted to see me again. I told him I passed by the bridge every day after school, and with that we left one another. I had spent two hours with him. He hadn't seduced me or even tried to. He had caressed me and told me there were many wonderful things we could do in the future. Then he gave me five thousand francs, and left. It was more money than I had ever seen in my life.

'Eventually I lived with him and was even sent to school by him. When my parents left Lyon he arranged for me to go to a boarding school where I would be well looked after. He had written to mother saying that there was a vacancy there for a term, paid for by some philanthropist. At that time, mother was only interested in my step-father and believed anything that left her free to be with him. My friend was a very rich man and though he arranged this school thing for me, I didn't live there.' She paused, then went on, 'Mothers only see what they want to see, don't we all?'

'So where did you live, Lily?' I asked.

'At his house and I went to a day school. Yet in the whole month I was there he never actually—I mean, he did a lot of things to me, but he left me a virgin.'

'And then what happened?'

Things became a little wild. He began giving parties at night for men and young girls and one day he was denounced to the police for interfering with minors. He sent me by aeroplane to Glasgow, where he had connections, and I spent six months there in a girls' school, and that same night he left for Switzerland. We didn't meet for three months, until I went to London from Glasgow to see him.'

'What about your mother all this time?'

'He fixed all that. He said I had won a scholarship. Poor mother! To think of her complete irresponsibility towards me, and that today I keep her. Yes, she knows what my life is and I send the money she lives on.'

'Oh yes,' she said, 'we all have a story to tell, you know. That's probably why Edouard and I are together and why he stayed with you.'

'How do you mean?'

'Because we are different from most people.' However, she did not know the nature of my relationship with Edouard. She knew I loved him, but wasn't quite sure about anything else.

The atmosphere had become friendly and confidential, almost intimate. Then suddenly, I asked her how Edouard made love and if he kissed her.

'When he bends down and kisses my neck and then my mouth I forget everything.'

'Do you make love every night?'

'Only when he wants to,' she said. He had said 'only when *she* wants to.' How could he kiss her. A prostitute was paid for putting her mouth everywhere—five pounds and put it there! And this boy, this beautiful creature, was kissing that mouth. 'Me! Kiss a prostitute! You're crazy!' Hadn't he said that only a week before? I shuddered at the thought. How could he kiss her when he knew where her mouth had been. That soiled mouth! I looked at myself in the mirror. I looked young for my age, extraordinarily young. The cheeks sagged a bit, the lines from the nose down to the mouth were drawn. Lily was nineteen years old, here was the face of a girl. And what about my mouth! Oh God! And I closed my eyes.

'Come here, Lily, I want to kiss you.'

'Moi?' She couldn't believe it. I went to her and kissed her on the lips, softly closing my eyes and seeing only Edouard.

The telephone rang and Lily spoke to a client. She told him she was free. 'He's the one I like best. He doesn't even touch me. He makes me put on special clothes. Oh God! La vie de putain! And then he does it all on his own. I wish they were all like that.' She laughed. 'Au revoir, Jo. Write down my number and don't dwell on hurting Edouard!'

'I'll try not to,' I said, 'and you try and see if you can't help me too.'

'I promise.'

The woman had a heart. Edouard was more of a tart than she. I couldn't think of her as a whore. I had referred to her as 'Edouard's whore' to Nem and Ricki . . . but she was nobody's anything. She was something on her own. Now what could I do to Edouard without hurting her?

During the next few days I had been bringing more and more people home. Sometimes the adventures were good, sometimes bad, but I never once knew what I had in my arms. I couldn't see them, I could see no one and smell no one but Edouard.

This evening, as I left Lily, I returned to an empty apartment.

I took a sleeping pill hoping it would make me sleep until morning. Instead, I dreamed that Edouard's suits which were in Ronnie's house (the ones he had in Paris when I knew him) were lying in a parcel somewhere in the basement and that they were ruined. They had a green mossy fungus growing over them. I could see it growing, spreading. It frightened me horribly. I awoke hysterical. I had to know if it was true. I dressed and ran down the five flights of stairs because the lift was busy. I took the underground to the other side of London to Ronnie's. I ran all the way like a fool, almost getting killed as I crossed the road as the cars flashed by. I ran into one that was pulling up. I looked round me like a hunted animal and then dashed feverishly along till I came to Ronnie's. I went straight to Edouard's room. It was being painted, the door had been replaced. It no longer smelled of him. I went to the back door. Bags and parcels were heaped one on top of the other and I heard a trickling of water. I couldn't believe it. From the wall near the ceiling, water was coming out of a hole in a continuous drip. This flow was falling right on top of the bags. I threw one after the other into the hall. Half of the things were sopping wet. A sad brown paper bag that I picked up fell apart in my hand and out of it fell a grey suit, a bright blue summer jacket and some shirts, all dyed the colour of the jacket. Edouard's! What did this dream mean. I felt bedevilled.

I had to find the boy, tell him what had happened, show him. He must see the clothes, hear the dream. I wanted him to realise what had happened, how much I cared for him and what I did for him. I took the dripping clothes into the street, over my arm until I was dripping too, then I stopped at the Greek shop where I got a plastic bag. I put his stuff into it and then took a taxi to his school. I would wait for him there. He would see me with these things I had saved and thank me and tell me I was his friend. I walked up and down in front of the school for an hour until he was due, and for another three-quarters after that, but he didn't appear. Now there was no way of finding him unless he was at the Voyous. So I went there. Only the sharp, thin-lipped woman, the one I had watched him make love to, was there.

'How can I find Edouard?' I asked.

'I am looking for him too,' she said. 'Tell him, if you should see him, to come at four instead of five.'

'All right,' I said, 'but I can't remember where his place is; where exactly is it?' She told me. At last I knew. It was difficult to find. He had not lied when he told me it was on top of the Golden Egg, but I couldn't have found it on my own. I dragged my dripping mass of clothes to the room and banged on the door. There was no answer, but it opened as I pushed. I saw Edouard's things and some of Michel's too. I longed to go through them. But I had no right to go through Edouard's things unless lovers have rights. I sat on the floor helplessly. I didn't know what to do. A weariness came over me. I wanted to sleep, I wanted that aching feeling to go. I took another taxi home, holding the parcel of dripping clothes in my arms, like some bleeding baby. I got to the flat and turned the bath on. The water ran fast and hot, but I gave up the bath until I had washed the clothes.

Then I counted, one summer suit, one summer jacket—the trousers missing—four white shirts of cheap nylon—and I was running all over London by taxi to show them to him! Edouard only wore turtleneck pullovers. London never had summer weather—what did he care about these old suits; he didn't even know he had them anymore. But I was insane. I felt I had saved them, saved him. He must be grateful, thankful. He must feel he couldn't do without me. I even remembered phoning him once in a rage, 'Either come and pick up your stuff or I'll leave it outside in the road.' He had not come back. So would he now throw himself round my neck for having saved these old clothes? But I had to save them and he had to know. When the bath was ready I stripped down to my underclothes. I threw the two suits into the warm suds. When it was over I let the water out, rinsed them and let them hang. Then I started again. More suds and bleach to get rid of the stains on the shirts. I was working feverishly; rubbing and panting, as if it were a matter of life and death.

The bathroom door was open and I was making one hell of a mess with flying soap suds and swishing water. I threw the shirts into the mixture and stood up to rub the sweat off my face with my forearm. My back was hurting. Suddenly I had a feeling that

I was being watched—I looked round. Edouard was standing there, smiling. He must have crept up silently. I felt weak. I was losing hold of myself. My knees gave way and I collapsed to the floor. Edouard caught me, patting my back as I slipped down through his arms.

'I'm sorry, I'm sorry, ce n'est pas du cinéma,' I stammered. 'I don't know what's the matter with me. I can't stand up, I can't.'

He stayed with me, kneeling on the bathroom floor, saying, 'Je suis là, je suis là.' I felt the end was coming. I was really going to break up, little bits of me falling off till nothing was left. Then I thought, I must do some terrible thing to him. But what and how and when? At one moment I felt tenderness, another hate. In return he gave me his absence or silence.

I looked at his bloodshot eyes. 'I want to take you to the doctor, I am worried about your eyes.'

'I went with Lily,' he said.

'It's not the same. I want to take you. I have my own ideas. What did they tell you at the hospital?'

'It's a form of conjunctivitis.'

'It should have cleared up by now. Please come with me!'

'No,' he said, 'I'm in good hands.'

'You're not, you don't do things right. You never returned to the hospital when you got that other disease. You are young and ignorant and unimaginative. That's why you're not afraid.'

'I asked my friend Alain to take over for me for a few days, but he doesn't want to. By the way, did you sleep with Alain?'

'How on earth can that interest you? He never asked me if I had slept with you.'

'I just wanted to know,' he said, 'to get an insight into Alain's character.'

'Then ask him.'

'I'd rather ask you,' he said.

'These are things one does not ask . . .' My voice trailed off. I let my head fall back to rest against the cool porcelain of the tub. I stayed there . . . sitting on the floor . . . until he left for work.

Chapter 24

I DID NOT SEE HIM AGAIN FOR THREE DAYS. BUT ALAIN CAME ROUND and we talked about Edouard. I told him exactly what our relationship had been. I was sick of protecting him.

Alain told me that everyone at the bar knew who I was. Edouard had even told them what I was.

'And did he tell them what he was?' I asked. 'Did he tell them he was a cheat and my lover?' How dare he explain me away as something from which he was almost entirely disassociated. He should have just kept quiet. Alain spoke a lot about Edouard and Michel. He told me they had invented a system by which they could steal a few shillings from the bar by not handing in receipts for the coffee. I asked if the owner knew and he said yes, that every evening he would ask Edouard how much he had stolen and they would have a laugh. How could Edouard do such a stupid thing? Money didn't interest him—he didn't want to save it or spend it, he didn't care about it. Why was he cheating the owners? All for a pound a week! What did it mean? Schoolboy naughtiness?

I was sitting home wondering if Edouard would ring when Ricki telephoned and suggested a film. I didn't want to leave the house for fear of missing a call from him, which Ricki guessed. 'Don't be a bore, he won't ring,' she said. 'And if he does, let him ring again. Come to the cinema.' The afternoon was a disaster. The film was depressing. It took place on a farm in Tuscany in the nineteenth century, all photographed through a heavy winter mist, and all infinitely sad. In the film the boy fell in love with a prostitute, just as Edouard had done. To take her out, he stole money from a till. There were scenes of violence and at one point he hit her across the face. I got all caught up in the film, identifying myself with it. I was the prostitute, Lily was the prostitute; he hit her, he hit me. I felt I was watching my own life. When it was over I left, unnerved and furious with Edouard. He had hit me, he had used me, he had hurt me. I would get even with him. Moreover, if he had left me, last time, on good terms, then it was part of his game. I would show him one could not kick people's hearts around; I would use a weapon he understood—expulsion. He excluded me, I would expel him, expel him from England.

The next afternoon I went to the room in Charing Cross Road, but there was no one there. I was certain I would find him and I knew he was friendly with others in the same building. I knocked at the door of a girl he had described as being like me, 'une hystérique'. There was no answer so I knocked again.

'Come in,' said a man's voice. It was a dingy little place, even smaller than his own. Edouard was lying in bed—he had been asleep. His eye was almost closed up and he looked sick. I laid my hand on his head.

'Fous le camp,'—get out, he said.

'I won't stay long, I want to be with you for a moment.'

'You bore me' he said.

'Be careful,' I warned.

'Je m'en fous,' he said. 'Je m'en fous, je m'en fous. I can't listen any more, I can't stand you any more. Leave me alone.'

I grabbed him roughly. 'Get up and come with me. I'm reporting you straight away. If you don't come, I'll ring them.' God knew who 'they' were or what I was going to do—bring in the policeman standing at the crossroads?

'I've thought of that,' he said. 'I'm leaving England. I'm going to Milan. I have a friend who works in a bar there.'

'My dear boy, by the time I've finished with you, you won't even get into Italy, you'll be watched even as you go back to France. Living off a whore is an international crime. You'll certainly be thrown out of England in a week, unless they imprison you. I've got you where I want you and I'll tear you to pieces.'

He lay in bed looking the other way, that poor eye watering. He looked so sad, so sick and I loved him so much. 'I will stop at nothing,' I continued. 'Your father is going to know everything, your brothers too. I'll even send photostat copies of that letter to the mayor of your village. God damn your soul! I'm not asking to sleep with you. You are pointlessly, senselessly, pitilessly detroying me—I am really dying.'

Something of what I said seemed to get through to him. Had I maybe finally touched him—just for a moment . . or was it perhaps he felt I might go into the street with him and start shouting for a policeman? He knew that then he would have to leave the country.

He got dressed slowly. It was raining. We walked down the Charing Cross Road arm in arm to my shoemaker and then to have tea. We must have looked funny—sick Edouard with his one watering eye and me with both watering.

'Edouard, all I am asking you is not to exclude me. Don't abandon me till I can take it and I cannot take it yet.' We walked out of the shop, again arm in arm.

'Je suis consterné,' he said. It was a funny word to use. But he looked at me with tenderness and suddenly hugged me in the middle of Piccadilly. 'I will phone you tonight from the bar.' That night he phoned as he said and promised to come the next day for lunch.

He arrived wearing a black patch over his eye and looked better. I loved him with the patch, he looked like a pirate. 'Climb through the window and attack me wearing that.'

'Lily said you'd love it!' he laughed.

The next evening I was to cook for friends at Nemone's. That afternoon Edouard came around and was sprawled on a chair as we chattered. His second eye had now become red and watery, but he was in a good mood. 'There are times I can't stand you and times I love you. I love you today,' he said. I didn't want him to leave. I looked at my watch.

'What about your work, Edouard? Look at the time.'

'Oh yes,' he said reluctantly, 'I'll go.'

Chapter 25

HALF OUR GUESTS FAILED TO TURN UP AT NEMONE'S THAT EVENING. It was disappointing. By eleven-thirty it was evident we were going to have a great deal of food left over. I suggested to Nemmie having Edouard and Lily over.

'No one will mind Lily,' said Nem. 'She's French and anyway, you know us. Provided a person isn't English, we can put it all down to being foreign! Ring them.' Lily went every night at this time to fetch Edouard at the bar. They would go home in a taxi. I telephoned and they told me she wasn't there.

'Then give me Edouard.'

'Edouard doesn't work tonight,' they said.

'The imbecile, he forgot,' I said.

'No he didn't, he didn't come. He knows when it's his night off.

The bastard! I was blazing with rage. I rang Lily. She answered sleepily. 'I rang up to ask you both to a party, Lily. I rang the bar where Edouard went after he left me—to go to work! But now I see he didn't go. Why did he lie? He's made a fool of me again. He is going to pay for it. I'm sorry you haven't succeeded in keeping your part of the bargain and I regret if you suffer as a result.' I hung up.

In my room that night, I wrote letters till four in the morning. I wrote to the Labour Exchange, to the Home Office, to his father, to the mayor of his father's village. I would finish him off for good. The cheap little bastard. It wasn't as if he had been bored with me sitting at home. It was I who had reminded him about his work and even then he hadn't seemed in a hurry to leave. Why this cunning and these lies? I started thinking about my revenge. The first thing was to get him thrown out of the job. I was full of poison, I couldn't see straight. I had to get my own back. Yet I didn't want to bring the authorities in—whatever I did—I must be able to undo also.

When morning came I tried to organise the traps, the plans for revenge that had run through my head during the early hours leaving me drawn and pale. I imagined a scene; he was accosted by a detective who asked him where he lived, what he did, who provided for him in London. Where he got his money and who was this woman he visited every night. I looked through the list of detective agencies. I rang. The first would give me no information on the phone, so I telephoned another. 'Could you please tell me the charges involved? This is my name. You can ring me back. I'm responsible for a French boy in London. He is working without a permit and not doing his schooling. His parents have written to me and they are worried he is in bad hands; they are thinking of having him sent back home. I would like you to go where he works and frighten him.'

'Don't worry, we'll get the boy back for you. Want him to come back, do you?' he asked. Oh my God, I thought. What have I done! I have told them nothing and yet the detective knows everything.

I must have hesitated, stammered. 'We weren't born yesterday,' he continued. 'Leave it to us. He'll be back at your place in no time.' I put down the receiver. I was shaking.

Chapter 26

AT MIDDAY I HAD A DATE WITH RICKI. I KNEW SHE WOULD BE ANGRY when she knew, but I couldn't keep anything from her. We met at the Hyde Park Hotel. She looked so grand and so important. Maybe I wouldn't tell her after all. 'You are beautiful,' I mumbled. 'You matter . . . some people matter.'

'Darling, what's the trouble? What are you talking about? What have you been up to? Tell me. Who else should you tell?' I told her. She listened and thought before she spoke. 'Can you get on to this agency?'

'Yes,' I said.

'Telephone them. Tell them Edouard's parents are arriving—that you don't need them. Tell them anything. You have already done too much.' I went to the phone and rang.

'I'm sorry I troubled you,' I said nonchalantly. 'I will no longer be needing you, I'm washing my hands of the whole affair. His father is coming to take his son away.' When I returned Ricki had tears in her eyes.

'The private detectives are all police who have been thrown out. They're often blackmailers. Do you know what can happen? You can fall into their hands for ever. What are you doing here with this boy? Are you having an affair with him? It's an offence in England.' She put her hand on mine, steady. 'You'd better leave, you'd better leave the country after all.'

After lunch I walked home. I stood looking into the Peter Jones window in Sloane Square and I heard Italian being spoken behind me. They were waiters from a Chelsea restaurant. 'Come and have some coffee,' I said, 'good Italian coffee.' I didn't want to be alone.

They said they would come later. One had to go round the corner and see about a job. 'A waiter's job?' I asked. 'Yes, waiter, barman, anything.' I went home and waited for them. In the meantime, I would try again to get Edouard thrown out of the bar. My flat was covered in paper. Thirty letters of hate and revenge lay around, all to do with Edouard, the result of a sleepless night. Should I destroy them? I could always write them again. I didn't—I left them ready to pop into a gaping letter box, that hungry red painted shark, standing with those open gashes, waiting to be fed. A dangerous weapon, the letter box. Letters, telephones, everything was dangerous! I rang Giulio at the bar.

'You know, you should lay him off,' I said, 'he's sick.'

'I can't,' he replied, 'I have too much work and there is no one here.'

'Don't say I didn't warn you, Giulio, I'll find you a replacement,' I said. 'I'll get him to ring you up in about half an hour. A good boy, with a permit—he's Italian, like you are.'

When the boys came I made the one still without a job ring Giulio in front of me. Giulio turned him down. The coffee party had been a waste of time and Edouard was still working at the bar—he had beaten me again. No sooner had the boys left than I rang the Labour Exchange. 'I have some information,' I said, 'about a man working without a permit.'

'We regret we can do nothing by phone,' they said. 'We have these anonymous accusations all the time. If it is a written complaint, we see to it immediately, not otherwise.' I said I would write.

Then Lily called. 'I have had no news from you since you telephoned me. How are you?'

'I am preparing Edouard's death. It won't be long now, Lily. He's going to be kicked out of the country.'

'Then I shall leave with him,' she replied.

'That's nothing to do with me,' I said. 'He has bitched me up and it's my turn now to bitch him up.'

'He's only a boy,' she said. 'You can't expect him to know what your feelings are. He is an irresponsible little animal.'

'It's my sanity at stake. What happens if the guard doesn't stop the train or the sailor on watch doesn't see an iceberg? Edouard is guilty of killing me.'

'You'll live to regret it,' she said. 'You'll live with it all your life.'

'Not if I can justify myself,' I said, 'and I can, I bloody well can.'

'He isn't at all well,' she said. 'Both eyes are bad now.'

'Not bad enough, he can go blind for all I care.' That's what I answered, but not what I was thinking. I was thinking of Edouard blind and now entirely dependent on me for giving him his sight back . . . I would get him an eye . . . no, I had one ready to give him . . . almost ready . . . a beautiful eye, I would give it to him one day. I owned a stone, a large square-cut emerald. My mother's but it would be mine eventually. I could have the stone placed in his socket instead of the blind eye. He would look fantastic. Edouard with an emerald in his eye socket. It would become a fable—every woman would want him. The man with the emerald eye.

Why shouldn't I let him go blind? Who wants a blind Frenchman? He would need me, he wouldn't be able to live without me. I would be the only one to remain faithful. What would his parents do for him? They'd find out he had some terrible disease, caught through his own vice. I was exhausted, I couldn't continue. I had blinded him, given him a square eye and now a disease. Gonorrhoea! That's what it was, I knew it was that. When I was young, a doctor had told me gonorrhoea blinds you within a few hours. Alright. He didn't have gonorrhoea, make it syphilis! Syphilis of the eye. But I didn't want him to go blind. Not because I loved him, but because he was beautiful. If he went blind and depended on me, the relationship would be different. Had I not done everything to see that he was independent of me? Yet I wanted him to need me. I didn't know what I wanted any more. I wanted him dead. I would find someone else. What had gone wrong? What? I had been too keen, too engrossed, too demanding, but it was too late to go into all that now.

'Are you there? Are you there?' It was Lily's voice over the telephone, anxiously repeating my name.

'Yes, yes, yes, I'm here. I was thinking.'

'You gave me a fright,' she said.

'What shall I do about Edouard?' I asked, miserable and aching for the boy I would go on loving even when I had destroyed him. Should I save him? He'd have to thank me then. He would say, 'I don't care for you the way you want, but no one has ever been to me what you have been to me. I shall never leave you.' That's what he would say, 'It's no good, Lily,' I said. 'He's going blind. He doesn't want me near him. Let him go blind, I can do no more. However, this is the last offer I make you. I am seeing Nem tomorrow. If he wants to come with me to the doctor, I will take him; if not, let him die and you can take your share of the responsibility.'

'Comment?' she said. 'How can you say that?'

'How do you know you didn't give it to him?'

'Give him what?' she asked innocently and sweetly and she was innocent and sweet.

'Gonorrhoea! You may have given it to him.'

'But I feel nothing!'

'You know nothing of such things, Lily. But I'm warning you, don't come to see me when it's too late. I can do anything—Edouard said so. I will cure him, I will save him. If not, he'll go blind; he'll die!'

Supposing it were true? Why wasn't he cured if it was a common case of conjunctivitis? It got worse each day. I remembered the sun shining in his eyes. The panther dots in green cat's eyes. Would I ever see them clear and arrogant again? A boy of twenty-one, a beautiful, healthy creature like that.

I don't know how I lasted till the next morning. I cannot remember where I went or what I did. I got to Nem's and telephoned Lily.

'He's coming,' she said.

'Tell him to hurry.' He arrived buoyant and handsome with his damaged eyes. No sooner had he entered the house than Nem's little daughter ran to him.

'Edouard!' she cried.

'Yes, that's right,' her mother said. He bent down to lift her in his arms. 'Please!' said Nemone, putting a restraining hand on the child as he was about to lift her up.

'Edouard, come here,' I said in French. We were standing in the kitchen and I walked him to the dining-room. 'She is afraid of your disease, you might make the child blind, you're a leper now. Even I wouldn't come near you.'

He hesitated. 'What should I do then?'

'Nemone has promised to drive us to the hospital this afternoon. Keep away from the child.'

'I can go alone,' he said.

'I know what you can do alone. I have seen you in hospitals. You waste other people's time and the government's money and you do nothing. You'll come with me and do as I tell you. Otherwise you leave England tonight. Originally it was your eyes I wanted to save, now I want to protect others from you. You cannot go around blinding innocent children. You're a monster without a conscience.' He didn't answer. We all went in Nem's van to the hospital.

I found a nurse and asked if I could speak to her. There were many people waiting and I was afraid Edouard wouldn't get the attention I wanted for him. 'Sister, this lad speaks no English and he has seen a doctor elsewhere. I do not know what he has. He doesn't even know what medicine they gave him. I am responsible for him in England. Will you personally see he's thoroughly examined?'

'There will be no nonsense when I'm around,' she said, 'leave it to me.'

'Let me know the moment you have news,' I told Edouard as I left. I got home and waited until five in the afternoon when his call came through.

'I have had every examination in the world,' he said. 'They have been so thorough—I even fainted at one point.'

'Are you all right?'

'Yes.'

'Do you know what you have?'

'They didn't tell me.'

'Did you ask them?'

'They didn't know. They are sending me to a specialist.'

'Don't you think it would be better if I came with you?'

'I don't want you to.'

'Have you rung Lily?'

'Yes I just rang her.' That's right, I thought—ring Lily first!

I rang the hospital the next day and talked to the sister. 'I am going to accompany the French boy to the specialist. I hope it will be alright. By the way, what's the nearest underground to the specialist? And his address? I fear he might lose them.' She told me and I wrote it down carefully. I then rang the bar again. 'Guilio, stop that boy from serving drinks with that diseased eye. Tell him the clients have complained. If you don't I'll see that they do complain. You have no right to employ him like that. You don't even know what disease he has.'

That night Edouard was laid off work by Giulio. Lily rang to tell me. 'That's better,' I said, 'He needs a rest anyway.'

'Yes,' she said. 'It will give him time to go and get his papers in order. He wants to prolong his stay here. His professor at school has taken his passport and Michel's as well and is going to get them stamped.'

No, I said to myself. No, not yet. He mustn't get permission yet. I want to kick him out. He'll have to go back to Paris and I'll go there too. He'll come back to me, then I'll find him that job in Air France and he will go to the sunny countries wearing his blue uniform and return to tell me of the whores in Bahia, the girls in Japan. I want him back, I want him back.

The next day was the day of the visit to the specialist. I would wait there for him. I went like a thief. I was afraid he might see me in the street. The building was a red brick forbidding looking place. I walked in—I was now the busy god-parent burdened with a tiresome responsibility. I asked for the doctor and they told me he was on the second floor. I stopped a tall man. 'I'm looking for the specialist,' I explained.

'What is it about?' he asked. 'He had an appointment with my godson, a French boy.'

'Solda?'

'Yes, that's it.'

'I'm looking after him myself,' he said. 'Have you a minute? It is very important that I speak to you.'

He showed me into a small room and closed the door. Now I would know all. I couldn't beat it if he said, 'Solda has a harmless nervous irritation, an allergy.' It had to be something terrible, something shattering. I wanted to use it, to show Edouard how I'd saved his life as I'd saved his clothes.

'What can I do for you?' he asked.

'That young boy is in my charge,' I said. 'I am worried about the life he leads and his health. What exactly is the matter with him?'

'He will be alright, I think. If he comes regularly for treatment. I think we can look after him.'

'What has he got that you think you can look after?'

'The boy is twenty-one; we cannot discuss his condition with anyone. I'm sorry I can tell you no more.'

'He would not be here today had I not made him come. Last time he went to a hospital it was I who made him finish his treatment.'

'Sorry, I can't tell you more.'

'What do I tell his parents? There will be expenses, I suppose.'

'There will be no cost,' he said.

'Doctor, why don't you tell me the truth? It's venereal disease—isn't that what he has?'

'I can tell you no more,' he repeated.

'Alright, doctor, if you can keep his secret, then you can keep mine. That boy is living with a prostitute, sleeping with her, putting his face down on her. Are you going to do something about that? If you don't tell me what he has, I shall know it's what I fear and I'll send him home. If he goes home, he won't have the treatment and he'll go blind.'

'He might,' said the doctor.

'That's terrible, terrible. How can you sit there behind a ridiculous professional secret when, if you shook him like a rat and made him bring her here as well, you'd save a population of whoremongers going blind too. Can't you use a bit of discretion, doctor, and do the sensible thing?'

'I can do no more. If you're worried about him, why don't you take him to a priest or a psychiatrist?'

'How can you, a doctor, say anything so futile? I am not against prostitutes, nor a man putting one's face there either, for that matter, I am merely trying to prevent half London getting a disease. Work it out; ten men a day, towels lying around, a drop of sperm and it's too late, isn't it?—or do eye doctors not know of such things?'

'I am a venereologist,' he said.

He said it, he said it—now I knew. Before I left I asked him another question. 'Doctor, should they make love in that condition?'

'Absolutely not.'

'Is there anything else you can advise? I want to help him and I want to help her. Can't you threaten to denounce him or something unless he comes for treatment?'

'I'm afraid I can't,' he said.

I left the room, walking out backwards. I don't know why I did, but I did. He must have thought me mad. What did I care? Let him think I was mad, mad about Edouard! I was saving dozens of people from venereal disease. Nothing the matter with madness like that.

The journey to Edouard's room in Charing Cross Road was a repeat of the one a few days earlier with the dripping clothes in my hands. The destination was the same and the blind precipitation with which I hurled myself across streets, on to buses, into taxis and out again was even worse. I had to see Edouard. He had to be there. I had to have my scene with him. I wanted to arrive, see him lying there eaten up by his disease and say, as he said to me when I had collapsed, 'Edouard, I am here, you will be alright, I will save you.' I would stretch my hand out, cover his eyes and weep. I wanted that scene, I had to have it. Now it was my turn. This boy who had kicked me around, broken me up, goes to live with a prostitute. I had stuck to him in spite of the insults and the scorn and had now saved his life. Shouldn't I get something out of it? I didn't expect him to fall on his knees before me, but I wanted some recognition. A look, a squeeze of the hand or even an insult given in a certain way, his way—'you stupid old interfering grandmother, mind your own business. I know you saved my eyes.' Was that asking too much?

I tiptoed into Michel's room. A figure was lying on the bed. It was impossible to tell who. Some brown hair showed and nothing else. They both had the same colour hair, both their clothes lay on the floor. Had it been a month before I would have known by the smell, but now Edouard no longer smelled the same. I got nearer and put my nose within a foot of his head. It was he. I stretched a hand onto his forehead. He was sweating.

'Edouard, c'est moi,' I said. 'C'est moi.'

'What do you want? Can't you leave me alone?'

'Edouard, I have something to say to you. I've been to the doctor. Do you know what you have? Did you know it was venereal?'

'I think so.'

'Have you got syphilis or gonorrhoea? That's what I want to know. Gonorrhoea—is that what the man said?'

'I think so,' he said.

'Well, my son, it is very serious. You can go blind with that! You should absolutely, without fail, have your injections and . . .'

'You must go,' he interrupted. 'My friend is arriving from Paris.'

'Why do I have to leave? It's Jean Claude. I know him. You spent your time in Paris telling me how he started to respect you when you started driving my car. Now you want me to leave because he's coming. You must get yourself attended to and bring Lily for an examination too. If you don't I will see that she gets reported. This is terribly serious. You can go blind; she can go blind.'

'Shut up,' he said. 'I'm so sick of hearing you talk.'

'Listen to me, damn you. I'm saving your life. I'm saving Lily's health. I'm saving every goddamn man who comes to sleep with her. You probably gave it to her. At least she knows about washing and keeping clean; she has some education. You are an ignorant Arab. Because I love you, it doesn't change what you are. You don't even know what you have—you aren't even afraid. You are an animal, an unfeeling, unthinking animal without a conscience. But I shall see you don't infect half this country as well.' Even as I said it I saw the absurdity of putting it on a national patriotic basis. I, the Englishman, saving the youth of England from Edouard and his tart's venereal disease!

There was a scuffling noise at the bottom of the stairs. Friends come to welcome Jean Claude from Paris. I put my hands on his arms, 'Give me some encouragement—let me feel I have done you some good.'

'Je m'en fous. Je me fous de toi, de mon œil, de tout. Fous le camp.' It was a bad moment. I thought of the many letters to the Home Office lying ready on my desk. If he wanted it this way, he would have it this way. I took a taxi home, ran up to my room, picked up a letter, stuck down the envelope and ran with it to the Post Office. I put it in the letter-box consciously, intentionally and without regret. As I did so, a curtain fell between us. Then I telephoned Air France and booked a ticket. I would leave. Edouard would be thrown out of the country and that was that. I lay on my bed, an inert mass of emptiness. I did not know how long I had been there. What was Edouard doing? He would know soon enough what had happened to him. If he needed me, I would be there. I would still find him a job, look after him, share all I had with him.

Chapter 27

THEN THE TELEPHONE RANG. IT WAS EDOUARD, HE SPOKE GENTLY, 'Jo-Jo, c'est moi Edouard—speak to me.' I couldn't stand it. I screamed down the phone.

'I can't . . . never, never again. I've betrayed you.' And I hung up. I burst into uncontrollable sobs and when that was over I lay on my face on the bed. An hour later, the telephone rang. It was Edouard again.

'Don't ring off,' he said. 'I want to talk to you.'

'I can't talk to you. I sent the letter to the Home Office. I sent it—I betrayed you.'

'Je m'en fous,' he said. 'I don't care about me, I care about you. I was abominable.' That was the word he used, abominable. 'Forgive me, I will come and see you.'

'Come now,' I begged.

'No, I can't. I am going out tonight with Jean Claude; it's his first night here.'

'When can you come?'

'Ring me at twelve tomorrow,' he said. I lay there wondering what would happen. What had I done? I hadn't really said anything awful in my letter. I had written I wanted no more responsibility, that's all. Not that he was a ponce, nor that he had a venereal disease, nor—yes I had. I had written that he was working, but I hadn't written where. However, he might get into trouble. I would try and arrange it; there must be a way.

The next day I telephoned at twelve.

Lily answered. 'He's asleep.'

'Wake him.' Lily woke him up. I heard him shouting. 'Tell him

I'll come later.' I put the telephone down angrily. It rang again. This time it was Clarisse and Richard. They had returned from abroad to spend the night in London.

'At my house,' I insisted.

They arrived—bags, child, governess—and the sad apartment began to live. How different it was to be with real friends, it was no longer a struggle of who can hurt the most, who can stand the silence the longest, who will make the first move. Richard went out to shop. I told Clarisse I expected Edouard.

'I had better leave,' she said.

'Are you mad, Clarisse? I would never put a lover before a friend, particularly a friend like you.'

At four o'clock there was still no sign of Edouard. It was unbelievable. Who could understand the boy? I couldn't and he couldn't understand me. 'Comprendre, c'est aimer,' to understand is to love.

At last I heard the squeak of rubber soles on the passage outside. I beat him to the door. 'What are you doing here?'

'You asked me to lunch,' he said. I would not let him inside the door. I was white with rage.

'It's half past five, Edouard. We went through enough yesterday. You told me to call you at twelve to wake you to come here to lunch. You're not working now, yet you come at five—get out!'

'You do all the talking,' he said and went off without looking back. I made an attempt to stop him. I think I ran to the lift but he had left.

Clarisse was terribly upset. She felt it had been because of her, but I would have none of that. 'It's terrible to make anyone suffer so unnecessarily. I feel like going to the bar and having a talk with him myself. After all, he's been to my house and I'm old enough to be his mother.' But nothing came of it. She had too much to do. I believe she might have arranged something since she saw his point of view too. She was the first to say I was mad, that my love for this boy was an unbearable burden. Any love that is not returned is unbearable. How many times had Edouard said, 'You mother me.' But now I was angry.

The next morning, ruthlessly and purposefully, I rang up the

Labour Exchange. I gave them all the information and I told them I had written to the Home Office. They promised to do something about it immediately. Lily rang up. 'I can't talk to you, Lily. I have reported Edouard.'

'I want to see you,' she said. 'Can I come tomorrow?' I asked if Edouard's passport was in order, if he had had his visa lengthened and she said she thought he had. Beaten again, beaten. But for how long? 'Je t'aurai,' he had said, 'I'll always get the better of you.' But not this time.

Meanwhile, I got different people to telephone the bar to find out if Edouard was working there again. Since he was, I rang the bar myself. 'Giulio, I warn you, get rid of Edouard. He has been denounced. Furthermore, you know where he is living. You know what it means to live with a whore.' (I did not feel I was betraying Lily since it was Giulio in the first place who had told Edouard about her.) 'Your bar is getting a bad name; it's only a question of days. I warn you, it may cost you an enormous fine. Get rid of him today!'

'I have no one to replace him.'

'Alright, Giulio, but don't say I haven't warned you. They are looking for Edouard.' I would ring the detective again, I would do anything to get even with him. Even have him beaten up if it wasn't that beating might ruin that face I still loved. What a nightmare! And only a few days till I left the country and still he was winning. The next day I rang the authorities again. With that same desire for revenge I began, 'These foreign kids think the Labour Exchange is run by a bunch of oafs, that you'll never catch him. Are you really a bunch of oafs?'

'We have written today,' the woman said sharply.

When Lily came to see me the following day, I was working at the typewriter. 'Edouard said he would give me a typewriter like this,' she said.

'Did he?'

'Yes.'

I was livid. So this bastard was going to give her my typewriter that I was keeping for him. I would tell him next time I saw him, 'This present is not for my pleasure, as you always accuse me, it is for you. Lily can buy her own. She only has to get down on her knees to three clients, that's all.'

'What's the matter,' Lily asked.

'Nothing,' I said. 'I was just wondering, forgive me if I ask you, but it is rather important. Do you still make love with Edouard?' She looked sheepish. For the first time since I had known her she irritated me.

'The doctor advised us not to, but of course you know, these things happen. I mean, we try not to.'

'In spite of what the doctor told you. Are you as ignorant as Edouard? Don't you understand what you can lose by this? I try to cure you, to save you and you look at me stupidly and say "we try not to" – once is enough you know.'

We talked and talked. Had I made love with him since he had been living with her? I hadn't. I asked about them and what they did together. It was a mad conversation. All we wanted to do was tell each other what we felt about Edouard. She told me he liked taking her the other way.

'He likes it, I don't. Some girls do, especially prostitutes, but it hurts.' She asked me if he made a noise when he came.

'Not a noise, Lily, a roar, a sob like a death cry. It's the most exciting, terrible thing.'

'So you know that too?' she said. I didn't tell her that he had stopped it lately. As I began to think about it I began to wonder whether even that part of Edouard was 'du cinéma,' to use his own word.

We were just two helpless people discussing the person we loved, simply and without embarrassment. I brought up the subject of his passport. 'Ring the bar and ask him if it is in order.' She telephoned. Only when she told them whom she was did they tell her what had happened. A letter had come from the Labour Exchange regarding Edouard. Everyone in the bar had been sacked. Edouard and Giulio had gone to a lawyer. There might be trouble. I sighed with relief—so things had caught up with him at last. I had no regrets. Let him rot. Then Rachel rang and when I told her what I had done she was angry.

'One cannot go to the Immigration Officer about one's love life.

I can't go to the police and tell them Ronnie is working without a permit or not paying his taxes because we have a lover's quarrel. You have done a terrible thing, dangerous too.' She rang me again at ten o'clock that evening and asked me if I wouldn't leave the flat and live with her for a few days. 'You might get beaten up there and we still love you.' I thanked her and cried. I had no more control.

Ricki was shocked. Jimmie the writer couldn't believe it. 'I'm taking you away. You're coming to America to help me finish my work.' Even my old friend Pamela, later, when she heard, wrote to me.

'Love is a mixture of sadism and masochism,' she wrote, 'Dostoievsky says so. But you! How could you—so kind and loving—have been so mad. No matter what he has done, to denounce him! In Ireland not long ago, one's life would have been forfeit. An informer is always killed.' She had written KILLED in capital letters and it was frightening to read. 'It will not get Edouard back,' she continued. 'He does not want to give up his independence. I know all's fair in love and war, but certain people will not see it that way. Only in the slave market can you buy a body—never a heart and a soul.'

I telephoned Murray in Paris. 'Come to Paris,' he said. 'You will finish by killing him or killing yourself.' Natalie said the same. Mirella wasn't interested in him. 'Waste of time,' was all she said.

I decided to leave Edouard and England.

Thanks to my letter to the Home Office, Edouard would be apprehended and expelled. There was nothing left to do . . . either for him or against him. Lily rang and asked what I intended.

'He should come round before I leave, we might try and arrange something.'

'I will tell him,' she said. Later Edouard telephoned. He told me that all the personnel at the bar had been sacked. They had asked about me and he said he did not know where I had gone. His lawyer had told Giulio that Edouard would have to leave the country. He never referred to what I had done, nor did he say anything to make me feel my guilt. He said he would come and see me on the eve of my departure. I said I was leaving at a quarter to eight and that he could come at four. By five o'clock he was not there. Everything depended on us coming to some decision, some plan to undo what I had done so he could stay in England to finish his studies and have treatment for his eye.

At five-thirty Lily rang. Had I any news? She had none—the same at six, still nothing. It was now nearly seven. I rang Lily again. She was worried something had happened to him. But he wasn't dead, no such drama. Oh God—let him die! Let him be dead rather than gone. Maybe they would find my name somewhere in his pockets and would ask me to identify him. I would hold his head in my arms forgetting he never wanted that, and I could sit there with him as he went cold. I would be the last one to touch him. At a quarter past seven I decided even if he did come I would not let him in. Could nothing to do with Edouard ever go right? I rang Lily to tell her; she did not know what to say.

As I put the telephone down, there was a knock at the door. I didn't answer, I lay there without making a sound. Then again. I still didn't answer, I didn't know whether he would leave or not. I didn't want to risk that, but I was furious with him. The telephone rang again. I told her he was outside the door. 'Let me talk to him,' Lily said.

'He can phone you from a public box. I am not having him here.'

'Ask him why he's late,' she said.

'Edouard,' I said, 'is there any reason why you didn't come earlier?'

'I didn't realise the time.'

'Yes, Lily, there is a wonderful reason, the poor boy never knew the time. Fuck off, Edouard, go away. Go and phone Lily from outside.'

'I shall stay here till you leave,' he said through the closed door.

He remained outside without speaking. Lily rang again. I repeated I would not let him in. 'Please do,' she said. 'He's not having a fight with me; he promised to telephone me and he didn't. He doesn't realise what he does. Let him in. Don't leave without seeing him.' I went to the door and opened it and just hugged him simply.

'Toi et ton cinéma,' he said.

'No, Edouard. It's your cinema this time, not mine. You have left us with only five minutes. How can I discuss anything with you now? Do you want me to arrange things with the Home Office?'

'If it's possible,' he said. 'Well, Jo-Jo, now that you're leaving, I shall be able to breathe at last.'

'You might also be going, Edouard, so shut up.' He smiled. 'I'll see what I can do,' I said. He didn't answer and did not seem to care. He had no imagination, that was the trouble. Why had he come? He hadn't even given me the chance to undo the harm I had done him. Before he left, we exchanged a long embrace. I need not have let out the stifled sob I did, but when he had his arms around me I gave in to that luxury on purpose. 'How do you know I will fix it for you?'

'I know you're not pretending. I felt your sob as you hugged me.'

The ass! The vain ass! I had done it on purpose to reassure him. I was quicker, sharper, more clever than he. But what did it matter? We weren't playing that game, we were playing another game and he had won.

What was I prepared to do for him now? The answer was everything. Everything provided he made it easy for me. He had made me suffer and I had done dreadful things to him. We were even. Maybe later on, when the strain and the pain had gone, he'd come to me. I had talked of spending holidays with him in Greece—we would row and swim and at night he could have his girls. I had it all arranged.

'Think of summer in Greece,' I said. 'I want to go with you. You will look well, all brown and strong standing on those rocks.'

'Je ne sais pas,' he said. 'If I go, I'll go with someone my own age, not with you.' As we walked away down the passage he looked round just as he used to do in the old days, when my day's happiness depended on it. But now, more than a day's peace or a night's rest hung on that smile. I was to be separated from him, maybe for ever. If he did not look back, I would not write the letter to the Home Office—he could sink. But he did . . . and he smiled the same insolent smile, the one I would always wait for and I forgot for a moment all that had been so painful.

I heard the lift—it would be Robert coming to take me to the airport. Was I ready, had I packed up everything? I must not leave things in drawers, as I always did wherever I went. I sniffed around the kitchen remembering I left a box with a dental plate in it. I had ordered it specially, in case I lost or swallowed the one I wore. I found later that I had taken a box of bicarbonate of soda in its place! Robert drove me to the airport. I was feeling light-hearted, my buoyancy was returning. England and my drama had cost me my honour, my health and pounds of weight. Now I was to be free again. I found a porter; 'The English are so kind,' I said to him in a ridiculous voice. 'Would you help an old man with a limp?'

'I'd help anyone with anything,' he said.

'For love or money?' I went on dottily.

'For nothing,' he said.

'Thank you, darling,' I said.

'Thank you, darling,' he answered in his funny, gruff cockney tone and took me to the stand to weigh my luggage.

There must have been a dozen girls sitting round doing nothing. Everybody's attention was focussed on me. The porter carried my stuff in and with a giggle said, 'Look after this darling 'ere.'

'That's me,' I said. Robert was dying with embarrassment yet amused.

'All this luggage for you?'

'All this,' I sighed. 'It's a long story. It's about "amour", you know. Anyone French amongst you?'

'Moi,' said one girl and then another, then another.

'I'll tell you. I have too much luggage and it's all because of that heart-tearing, ball-breaking pain, the pain of love.' They started to giggle, I lifted my hand to silence them. 'I also am laughing on the outside, but inside I'm crying. How much extra luggage have I?'

'You have thirty-five kilos.'

'That's right, that should have been on the ticket of the one I love,' I said, looking at one of my trunks.

'Go off with someone, did she?' asked a funny friendly little cockney.

'No,' I said, '*He* did! He went off with a pretty, pretty girl and left me with the luggage to pay.' There was a second's consternation and then everyone laughed. Then one girl gave a loud hiccough which sent them all off again. I dived into my pocket for my packet marked 'Bicarbonate' in big letters and without a word I put it in front of the girl. I paid no overweight.

In Paris I went to the garage and got into my car. It looked splendid and I felt different sitting in the driver's seat after feeling the world had been sitting on me. I sent a letter to the Home Office: 'Sir, I wrote to you concerning E. Solda last week. Since this letter his parents have scolded him and he has been enrolled in another school. There has been a change of faith and I am willing to continue guaranteeing him. At twenty-one, without parents nearby, one is little more than a naughty boy! Yours, etc.' But even though I felt better now, deep down in my heart there was still poison, because I distinctly remember, as I wrote the letter, wondering what I could subsequently write to them if Edouard upset me again.

I telephoned Lily from Paris and spoke to him. He wasn't unpleasant. I sent him underclothes he wanted and received no thanks. I wrote and asked if he had received them. He answered, 'I am writing you for one reason only—to avoid your having more hysterics and causing more trouble for us all. Since you left, Giulio has set the whole of the Soho underworld on your track. I say I know nothing of your whereabouts. I am glad you left. I can breathe at last. If you must write, write to the bar.' The letter upset me. I telephoned London. He was not much more comforting on the phone, nor did he mention my parcel to him.

Lily, on the other hand, was nice. She kept me informed about him and wrote in English. 'Dearest, I know you like to have my letters because for you there is something of Edouard in them. He will write, but he must be in the mood. I am glad you realise the few months you spent so unhappily in London were only a small part of your life and not the whole. I fear so much the thought of losing Edouard and although I have deep feelings for you, in a way I fear you more than a woman, because you are special and Edouard is special and no ordinary person would suit him after two like us. I do not know his feelings about going to Paris for a few days, but believe me, I'm not ready for it. I think it is better that he does not go. I am not happy because I fear you want him back. You cannot ask me to send him back to anyone. I feel bad that you think I am trying to keep him.'

She was right, contact with her was contact with him. In her next letter she wrote, 'I have decided not to try to know about Edouard's thoughts anymore. I keep him like water in my hands. As long as it lasts so he will last. I am grateful for each day together. It is no good hoping for the day after tomorrow.' Her next letter said: 'I was happy to get your news. Do not suffer anymore—you suffered too much. I have little to tell you, but I love to talk of him. He is so sweet, so gentle, of course he never gives me any guarantee. This afternoon he said I was responsible for him. I do not think him strong. He needs someone. For the moment it is me and I love him. We are still under treatment. The pills make us tired, but we are well. Hope you are over your great sadness.Toujours, Lily.'

She wrote faithfully, but Edouard stopped writing altogether. I started to smoulder again. I had a terrible streak of nostalgia that night. I lay in bed twisting and turning and after a painful attempt to sleep, I turned on the light and looked around the room. I stared at the ceiling and recognised the stains that Edouard had made when he threw the peach at the wall the first day we met. That was six months ago. I stepped on a chair to touch them. The hardened bits of skin had formed a crisp, black crust. I was back in my state of hate and revenge. I telephoned Lily to threaten Edouard with more trouble if I didn't hear from him, but she wasn't in. I waited till the next day and put a personal call through to Edouard himself. I heard Lily saying nervously to the operator, 'I don't know when he will be back, he may not be back, not tonight, I am not sure.' I went mad with rage.

This time they were in for it, both of them. I would give her one last chance the next evening because she had trusted me. I wouldn't play her a dirty trick. I would try not to involve her, but I would get to him. I sat on my bed and simmered. I visualised them lying there, she, a long cigarette between her long fingers, his head on her breast, and the telephone ringing. Edouard's sensual mouth would say: 'At least we're spared the pain of seeing Jo as well as hearing him. Viens, kiss me; tell me you love me.' Turning to her as she still held the telephone in her hand, the cigarette smoking away, he would kiss her while she said into the telephone, 'I don't know when he will be back, maybe not tonight or tomorrow.' People who steal are evil, I thought, but murder I can understand. The French are right. Jealousy and love are good reasons for murder. I buried my head in my pillow and wanted to die.

I drugged myself to sleep. There were no letters the next day and when I returned, just before I put another telephone call through I got a special delivery letter from Lily. I had spent the afternoon plotting their doom, both of them. I opened the letter written in English, tearing it in my frantic haste. 'Dearest, I have no words to tell you what happened. I do not believe it yet. Edouard has left me. It happened last night. I decided to go to the bar. I had a premonition. When I feel like this something always happens. At eleven I saw Edouard coming to the Voyous. He went into the phone box and saw me there. What do the details matter. He had been going with that girl for sometime. I am hurt, so hurt. I said too much. He came home and I told him to pack and leave. He is not coming back. There is something dead in me now. I feel he will never come back. I did not work today. It does not matter anymore. Lily.' The letter was pathetic. What misery, what emptiness she felt. What would happen to her now? She would go through what I went through only it wouldn't be so bad for her. I was forty, she was nineteen. But was that true? Who knows for whom it was worse? What did my love mean? Everything. I would take a job and get up at six—a thing I have never done—What was she willing to do? I had asked her once as she sat in my room.

'Would you give up your easy life, your five pounds for ten minutes or whatever you get, and earn three pounds a day instead? Would you, for him?'

'He has never given me the choice. Maybe if he wanted it I would, but he hasn't asked me.'

I wrote to Edouard at the bar, but received no answer. Then, five days later and quite unexpectedly, I got a letter. I knew as I opened it that I was still hideously, hopelessly, and helplessly involved. The letter was thick and I wondered what it contained. I read it greedily. 'I found some letters of yours waiting for me at the bar yesterday. You may or may not know by now that I am no longer with Lily. Sooner or later, as I told you, we would have to part. I told her this a few days after we started living together. In fact, I already had one scene with her and I told her it would be better if we left each other then, but she begged me to stay so I stayed. If I deceived her into thinking I would be there for good, it was just one of those mistakes. She had this last scene with me because she saw me coming to the Voyous with a girl I had been going with for some time. When we got back to our flat she wanted to know about it and I told her.

'This other girl's Jewish too and has a remarkable body but doesn't speak French.' Here I had to giggle. The letter continued: 'Lily asked me where we had come from and I told her we had been to a room. When I saw in what a state she was, I left her. I didn't take my things—maybe because I wanted one day to return, I don't know. You see, if I had already thought of warning her we would break up one day, something must have been basically wrong from the start. Lily is a prostitute; I considered her a normal girl, which is the way she wanted me to consider her, so she could be loved by me. When I made her break up her affair with her Swiss boy friend, and took his place, she was very pleased. That was my mistake. I should have been a ponce to her. I should have seen to it that she bought me things and took me out; but that is not what she wanted. So I played her game, gave her a little love, and got tangled up in the game myself, only to come to the conclusion that a prostitute cannot sentimentally love a man like a normal woman. I am as I am. If I have some value, the only person to ever see it is you, but you are blinded by your hysterical obsession. Everything you wanted to make out of me fell apart. If it has given you material for a book, go ahead and write it. But I am far more simple than all that. You ask me to write my version of the story—not a bad idea. And when people read my version, they will also see the value which I know you have.'

If Edouard thought, after all I had done, that I had this 'value', then there was hope. Something might still come of it. He might come back or come to Greece or something. I couldn't be on bad terms with him. I couldn't. He must either be my friend again, or I would kill him! And if I did kill him, what would I do with a dead

Edouard? He would no longer be my Edouard. I sent him some money to buy Lily a Sign of David, an emblem to put on a chain. She wrote and thanked me almost immediately—which surprised me and said she still had no news of him. I then telephoned him daily at the bar—the answer was always the same. He was not working at the bar. He was away—they thought he might be in France. I couldn't understand it. Why then, the letter full of confession and detail, so dangerous and compromising? If he didn't trust me, why had he written? Why? If all he wanted was to get rid of me? Should I really believe he hated me? If I had some consistent behaviour to go by, I might take a stand. But I never knew. A letter from Jimmie in Hollywood decided me. I'd leave, join Jimmie in another continent, where I could not even telephone Edouard! I had lost. I must leave.

I went out and walked and walked, and when I returned, another letter from Lily had arrived. 'Dearest, the anaesthetic has worn off. I am feeling the pain. He cannot return to me after what I told him. I don't know how to get him except at the bar. Perhaps he couldn't stand the thought of all the men I see. Perhaps he had to leave for a while. It is not his fault. I told him to go. I hate to be alone, to sleep alone. It is hard for me this solitude. The way he went, so easy! Like the way he came! He fell into my life and now he is there no more. Every day when the phone rings I hope for his call. I wait for the last underground. I don't know if I even want him anymore. Maybe it is better to leave him be. I must do as you say, put money aside and start another life, and yet, if he were here to hold me in his arms and kiss my neck . . .' She wrote often. The rest of her letters shorter and more resigned, but still no news from Edouard.

Chapter 28

A TELEPHONE OPERATOR WORKING IN MY HOTEL HAD BECOME MY friend. She used to pop into my room and talk—she was bright and young and I liked her. I had soon related the whole of my drama to her, so she gave me an address in Switzerland saying, 'Send a specimen of his handwriting and have it analysed.' I left before the answer came. Against everybody's advice, I decided to go to America via London. Murray warned me I would only hang around the bar and it would all start up again. On arrival in London I did all I could to find Edouard. I got a girl to call the bar for me and ask about him. They said he had gone to France. I went to the girl in whose room Edouard used to hide from me, in Charing Cross Road. She said he was in France too.

That evening as I was about to cross the street a burly man stopped me. He was a little drunk. 'Where can I get a drink at this time of night? I don't want to go to bed yet.' I took him home. He had a glassy look in his eyes and it excited me. I provoked him and made him drink and then it happened. It happened with the added excitement of doing something I felt troubled him. He looked at me defiantly at one moment and asked. 'Do you know what I am?'

'You're a police officer,' I guessed. He didn't answer, but slowly took something from his pocket and handed it to me. It was a Metropolitan Police card. I stared at it, neither of us spoke and I walked up to him.

'Rub me with it!' I said. He did. His glassy eyes stuck to mine as he rubbed the cold dead thing over me. Then with a start we both stopped. There were footsteps at the door, then a knock. I was petrified. Was it some trick he had arranged—hadn't I enough to contend with without the police? I didn't answer. Then my name was called.

It was a woman's voice. Lily.

'Let me in,' she said as I opened the door. She stood there, her strange face, flat . . . expressionless. 'I feel so alone,' she said. 'Can I sleep the night with you?'

'Of course,' I said, though I didn't want her. I was happy with the policeman, I hoped she would change her mind and leave. I took her to the kitchen. I thought of Edouard who had thrown a jinx on me, interrupting me when I was with the Negro in Paris. Now somehow he was doing it again.

'I have no one to talk to,' she said. 'I . . .'

'It is worse for you than for me, Lily. I can talk to everyone about it. I drive them mad. I know—But I can't see you telling your clients! But at least you have been together and you are young and pretty. You will be having other things in your life. I will not.' The policeman interrupted occasionally with 'Wouldn't mind doin' 'er!' It was funny. I had told him she spoke no English, that she was a student, although I must say walking into the room at night on those long, luscious legs, her enormous breasts covered by a white embroidered blouse with pearls and silver all over it, she didn't look much of a student. After a while she felt better and left. He stayed and worked on me—rather wonderful. I slept late till the postman woke me with a registered letter.

It was a cheque from home. I jumped with joy. 'I can take him to America now . . . buy him a ticket and he would stay with Jimmie. Jimmie would find him a job in films. He would earn enough in a month or two to make the first payment on an apartment, the flat I had always wanted him to have. He'd be a success. Even as a failure, if he worked for a few months, he could have a few thousand dollars in the bank. That was a wonderful sum. I wrote an express letter to the Voyous, to be forwarded. I sent a copy to him at his father's address, also to his father. I told him that Jimmie had a free ticket which a film company had given him for a secretary. If he agreed to come to America, he must answer by telegram. I cabled the father saying I would telephone him on

Sunday morning at the village Post Office, but when I put the call through there was no one to accept it. I felt completely stumped from every angle. There was no one to turn to—no way out—I was beaten and he was gone. . . . forever.

Chapter 29

THE DAY BEFORE MY PLANE LEFT FOR AMERICA, I RECEIVED THE report from the graphologist in Switzerland. I rang Lily and told her. She insisted I go there. We talked of nothing but Edouard. There was nothing new to learn. Lily again told me how he made love to her in a way she didn't like and it hurt. On leaving her, I telephoned Rachel and told her what Lily had told me.

'There you are!' said Rachel, 'That proves what I've always said. Edouard likes men!' In the meantime, we went through the letter from the graphologist carefully. I considered it a brilliant analysis at the time, although Murray months later said it was rubbish. The heading was, 'Concerning Case Ed' and then it continued, 'Sensitivity. Psychological level superior to most.' (Murray asked me what that meant.) 'Modern type with refinement on one hand, very primitive qualities on the other.' It went on haphazardly making vague statements in foggy words, 'amateurish, adaptable, opportunist. Realism mixed with superficiality, disdainful, well under control, appears harder than he really is. Like a cork floating on the water. He thinks he is independent but he is both vulnerable and easily influenced. Totally undisciplined. Inability to finish anything, relies on the imbecility of people to be looked after, seeks neither self-advancement nor security, looking for an easy way to get by and can adapt himself to any situation. An animal that wants everything from society and wants to give nothing in return. He wishes to receive, assert his own personality and doesn't give a damn for the rest. Intelligence: type—conceptual.' Murray was so mad here. 'What's that idiot talking about. I don't want to hear any more.'

I thought it was wonderful at the time and every French word like 'conceptual' that I didn't understand, I put down to the genius of the graphologist. Furthermore, he had also said that Edouard's judgement was 'sure and penetrating.'

Lily begged me for a copy before I left. Together, in front of all those big blown-up pictures of Edouard, we sat underlining the things I disliked most about him. By the time I had finished it I had a perfect picture to present to his father. I had the pages photostat-copied. Then unexpectedly the next morning, I received a letter from the Home Office, forwarded from Paris. It informed me that, due to my second letter, they had decided to let Edouard stay on in England. I photostated this as well and sent the whole lot to his father. Before leaving for the airport, I telephoned Edouard's bank. I had been there when he had opened his account, was it not my cheque that had opened it for him? I spoke to the girl in that department and told her I was the godfather of Edouard Solda, that he was away for a week, and that his parents had asked me to see that he had sufficient money in the bank as they had no news from him. I had told him to open the account and I asked her how much he had left. She was unwilling to tell me, it was against bank regulations.

'Oh my dear,' I said, like some benevolent old uncle, 'of course I wouldn't dream of asking you to be indiscreet. I just have to know if the boy has enough to go on with, failing which I will come round and add some more. He is quite irresponsible and I want to help him.'

'In that case,' she said, 'I wouldn't worry. He has a good half left.' That was all I wanted to know. Edouard must be returning to England finally.

I wrote to him saying that his refusal to answer my letters had lost him a job in films and at least a thousand pounds. I sent him a copy of the letter from the Home Office and told him I would go on writing to him, that I was his parent, a parent who had chosen him, and that when he got tired of kicking me around I would appreciate a little kindness. Then I left for the airport. I sat for half an hour thinking of what I had left undone and decided to call up Giulio at the bar and apologise. By then I was on the verge of tears.

'Hello, Giulio. This is me, Jo . . . I am leaving the country in five minutes. I'm ringing you to apologise from the depth of my heart. I beg you to forgive my treachery. You do not know how many months of strain I suffered before I did this vile thing. I warned you, you know. I telephoned you three times so that you would get rid of him and you didn't. I have a terrible conscience about you.' They were shouting out the number of my flight. 'Giulio, you don't know the things he did to me. I looked after him. Don't think I blackmailed him to go to bed with me, I didn't. He had but to be a little kind and there would have been no trouble. He did the same to Lily as he did to me. He's a heartbreaker. Right now, I'm so desperate about him I am liable to get him into trouble with the International Police.' I had said this with the purpose of keeping them all afraid of me.

Giulio replied, 'I hold no rancour towards you.' The word stuck in my mind. He asked me if I had signed any statement about Edouard working at the bar, since till then there had been no definite proof and he had to know how he stood with the law about having employed Edouard (and for my sake I had an ironic afterthought). I told him I had sent a private detective but I had not asked him to testify, therefore the Home Office had no real proof that Edouard had been working there. I was glad to ring off. I felt abject.

In America Edouard disappeared from my thoughts. I didn't discuss him because I didn't feel the need to, nor had I any desire to return to Europe. But Jimmie's home by the sea at Malibu was perfect . . . alas, for the return of my neurosis. While he was away working I stayed home with nothing to do, so I would sit down and write out my story. As I sat in the sun alone at a round wooden table by the sea, I heard children laughing and shouts of wild young surfers being hurtled into the foam. I would suddenly fold up double, my head in my hands, whispering, crying out, 'Edouard, Edouard, where are you?' I could, of course, get in touch with him by denouncing him again. But whereas the first betrayal was understandable, the circumstances forgivable, no one would ever speak to me if I did it again. There was nothing I could do but weep and work and forget. I was told it wouldn't pain me for more than a year. There was another six months to go. I could stand it—weep a bit more and sleep a bit less.

For a week the madness was upon me. I dreamed that Edouard had come and was accepted for a film. Everyone liked him, all those girls, those pretty, healthy, long-legged American beauties, each with her own sports car and rich parents in Beverly Hills. They adored the Frenchman. I even found him a wife, lots of wives. Edouard was all set for a wonderful future, home, car, a job, children, everything. I did it all, I did it. Then I would be exhausted after having arranged it all—the girl in her white dress with her fine background, Edouard with nothing but his ambiguous smile, his indifference, his rolling shoulders. I'd buy him that 'Pour un Homme' again. He'd smell like he used to, and occasionally he'd come to Malibu where I was, even after he was married, and we'd talk and he would put his arms around me and say 'Sacré Jo, you did it all for me.' And I'd believe it and I would lie in the sun, smiling happily.

On another occasion I saw Edouard married to a pretty girl. This time I wasn't there. Who needed me anymore? I'd prepared America as I'd prepared England for him. They were expecting a child now. They still didn't want me. Hadn't Edouard told me he wanted to be rid of me in England? It would be no different in America. There would be no place for me. Alright then, I'd go to the south of France—his father would know where he was and I could see him, threaten him. We would send a telegram to Edouard, 'Mother sick, come.' I would be there; the mother would help me and Edouard could get the apartment I wanted to give him. The French love money, everyone loves money. I would buy them all, but I couldn't buy Edouard and now I had spent all my extra money anyway. Once I had said to Rachel, 'If only he were a bit of a whore, I could deal with him—I would simply buy him.' Rachel said, 'If he were one he would be with someone much richer than you. Take only what he is willing to give. La liberté de chacun s'arrête là où celle des autres commence.'

There was nothing I could do but go on writing him every month. And then, out of the blue, a postcard. No, this wasn't a dream. I showed it to Jimmie. A postcard from Lily.

'I am so happy. I had a postcard from Edouard. He is in Nice. So Edouard wrote to Lily. Edouard has written a postcard without an address, to a prostitute in London from whom he was separated and who has not seen him for three months. Therefore, I, Jo, have something to live for—I can breathe, I can live again. I must go to London, I must go to France. I must see him or I shall die. I wrote a happy long letter to Edouard at the bar and sent a copy care of his father. I also wrote a following letter to his father telling him to open Edouard's letter and contact him.

'Edouard: It's been such a long time since I saw you. I have so much to tell and so much I want you to tell me. I am arriving for a day or two in London on September the first, then I will be two days in Paris. After that, Florence at the Majestic Hotel. I am going with Jimmie and his girl friend. Contact me at any of these places. We are driving to Greece. You will see two wonderful new countries and you can do as you wish. I want you to do the driving, which you do admirably. What fun to end these painful months with a happy holiday, together. As always.'

He would answer, of course he would. I would find him. There was no time to get an answer here, but I would start looking in London. All would be well. Eight days later I was flying back to London. I must get back to Edouard. I looked out of the window. 'We are now flying over Belfast,' they announced. 'We will be at London Airport in little over half an hour.' The sky was ablaze, a mass of flame licking into the bright turquoise of the dawn. The inferno we were coming into was not up in the skies, but down there where there is life, money, traffic, agony, death! And look what one must go through to get there, to Edouard, to my world, my blind, driven world. The little world of Edouard Solda was all I cared about after forty years of living and travelling and reading and learning and seeing friends die.

I stepped off the plane into a long, sad London drizzle. I went straight to Nemone's. First thing in the morning I telephoned Lily. She had had no further news of Edouard. She was better, she was no longer in such pain. She asked how I was and I told her worse than before. She asked me to come over, but I was leaving the next day for Paris so I didn't see her. I telephoned Giulio at the bar. I told him who I was. I told him I had to find Edouard, it was very serious.

'It's worse than before,' I said.

'In case we have news, give me your telephone number and I will ring you,' he answered. I spent the morning out and returned to Nemone's for lunch. She was standing at the door waiting for me.

'He's coming,' she said.

'Who's coming, Nem?'

'Edouard.'

'No, no, it's not true, Nem, it's not . . .'

'We don't joke about such things,' she said tenderly, putting her hand on my shoulder. 'He said he would telephone, he wasn't joking, he'll come. Now I must go out. I will be back at five.' I did not wait long. The telephone rang and I picked it up and Edouard spoke to me.

'C'est toi—is that you?' he said laughingly, friendly.

'Yes, of course it is. I'm only here just today. Come quickly—I long to see you.'

'Are you alright?'

'I will be after you come round. Don't get killed on the way—I couldn't bear it. Not till I've seen you, anyway and I have news for you.'

'Good or bad?'

'Bad,' I said. 'I still love you.'

'Sacré Jo.'

I was alone in the house when he arrived. He was less handsome and his smell had changed. He wore my black shoes, the blazer I had given him, and his hair was different. He had it cut off, because as he explained, he now had a job as a croupier in a gambling club and he had to dress in dark clothes and look serious.

'No more turtleneck pullovers?'

'No.'

I sat on the floor next to his chair. He put his hand on my head, he patted me, and he hugged me. I didn't know or care if he meant it. Now that I come to think of it, maybe he was scared I would start denouncing him again. I didn't mind the reasons. He was there.

'Well, my boy, maybe if I hadn't lost you your job you would still be earning ten pounds a week at the bar instead of the thirty you are earning. Now, of course, there is no question of your coming to Greece. Another year maybe. Why not? You could have made good money in America,' I continued, 'You'd have made a few thousand dollars in the two months we were there and you would have paid half an apartment in Paris by now.' Edouard couldn't believe it.

'You mean you could have got me a job?'

'I had a job for you,' I lied. 'I had it. Even if you had been a failure, you would have been an extra and living for nothing in wonderful circumstances at Jimmie's. You'd have changed your category, your class, everything.'

'But how?' he asked. I was not telling him a complete lie. I could, I know, at least have gotten him the job of extra with the company Jimmie was working for.

'How could you do that?' he asked.

'Because, you ignorant bloody fool, I can do it over a cup of tea, you ass, you Arab, you imbecile. Because that is what connections are for, because that is how you get on in life, through other people.'

I asked him if he would return to see Lily. 'Oh, you know, living with her all day long!'

'Be kinder, Edouard. Youth is not kind because youth does not understand. There is no word in French for kind.'

'I can only judge by what I suffer and I have never suffered from that sort of thing.'

'You are lying, Edouard. You saw me collapse, you saw me hurl my head against the wall, you saw me jab scissors into my arm. You do know how much I cared and you did not give a damn. I could have done worse to you to avenge myself, you know.' He thought for a moment before answering.

'Jene suis pas franc,'—I am not frank, he said. A grave admission for a Frenchman.

I asked him about his father. 'I have not heard from him,' he said. 'I went to stay at home then I went to Nice. When I returned to London, I received a letter from him. He must have heard something about you or guessed what it was all about, for he wrote saying I was a disgrace to the family and he did not want to hear from me if I was that kind of boy. It was the last I heard of him.'

'Bring me the typewriter,' I said. 'Dear Mr. Solda:' I wrote. 'I have just seen Edouard who is well. I regret you have had words with him. Edouard has made me angry on several occasions. He has been disappointing. As his father, you are not there to judge Edouard on what I write about him. On whose side are you? On the side of people you do not know, or on the side of your son? You have attacked him without proof and without hearing him out. Edouard is lazy, arrogant, even callous; but I remember he gave me his money when I had none. He never asked for a single thing when he was with me and refused everything I wanted to buy him. Write him. Tell him that whatever he has done you are and always will be his father and his friend, that you will criticise him, curse him, and reprimand him, but that you will always love him. He is your son.'

I put the letter down. 'If you have lost your father, Edouard, let me take his place? He only made you, I chose you.' It was time to go. I kissed him and watched as he grimaced and wiped it pointedly off his face. This was a good sign, part of our game. I pulled his head towards my shoulder, just like old times, and he let it drop, like a dead head. All that was missing was seeing him curled up in his bath.

'Look,' I said, showing him a fat book of loose papers tied up in a blue cardboard folder. 'That's my manuscript. The story of the anguish and heartache of our relationship. You told me once you would add your version to it.' I gave him my address in Greece and asked him to write. I watched him leave through Nem's window and run for a taxi. As he got in he turned and smiled at me. And he was gone.

I drove with Jimmie to Geneva and the following night we arrived in Florence. I reorganised my luggage there. What happened next I wouldn't believe. My manuscript was missing. I telephoned Geneva and wrote to every restaurant, garage, where I might have left it. I also wrote to the hotel in Paris. There was no way of knowing if it had been found or not . . . but since it was of absolutely no possible interest to anyone else, I was certain I would either find it on my return to the hotel in Paris or elsewhere. So I stopped thinking about it. I wrote Edouard, short lines and postcards. I told him in a letter from Florence about losing my manuscript. I knew he would appreciate the significance of it. Then I sent him that funny postcard from the Palazzo Vecchio depicting two huge bearded wrestlers. One holds the other round the waist upside down squeezing him to death, while the victim tightly grips his assailant's penis. They both have expressions of agony and ecstasy. I could not resist the temptation of sending it to the bar. On it I wrote, 'This can also happen to you!'

Greece was superb. At every lonely rock, every swim in some deserted cove, every trip to the wild dervishes of the Pacific Club, I thought of Edouard. I received mail, but none from him. There was a postal strike and maybe his letters had fallen into one of those dismal post office bags. I left Greece with no news of either him or Lily. But I had given up the fight. I had no spirit left to go on. It was over, I could do no more. If he didn't want to contact me, I no longer had any excuse to contact him. Still, I bought some pullovers for him in Rome and we all drove back to Paris.

On arrival there I asked if there was any mail and they handed me a stack of letters. There was nothing from Edouard. If there was no news of him I would give the box of things I had bought for him to the night porter. Lily did not know I had seen Edouard in London because he had asked me not to mention it. What had I to say to her now that Edouard was no longer a link between us? Her life was a series of adventures; what men paid her, what they wanted from her, how they wanted her to dress up, or dress down, or talk French, or sing. There was a limit to what one could listen to. Yet I did care for Lily. I wrote to her the same night. 'Dearest—just back. Alas, no news from you or Edouard. I bought him some things in Rome, but since I heard nothing from him, I gave them all away half an hour ago. Tant pis! That is not the only drama—I have lost my manuscript. I will never find it. All those tears, that pain, the months of work, typing, retyping, reliving the horrors of this last year. Well, there's nothing left of it at all. Not one single line. Maybe it's all for the best. I could never do it again. Je t'embrasse.'

The next evening I got a telephone call from Lily. 'You are back! I wrote to you in Greece and so did Edouard. But then you don't know the news—he is back and we are together. Here he is.' Then he came to the phone.

'Hello, Edouard. I had lost faith in you. No matter! I still love you.' He laughed and said he might come over and see me. Two days later I received a batch of letters forwarded from Greece. There was one from Lily and one from Edouard. Lily told me she was so happy because Edouard had come back to her, and then she asked me if I had arranged it. The other letter was typical of Edouard. He refused to show he was happy about finding Lily again. He wrote in that tough style that bored me. It might have been a letter to Michel, not me . . . 'Mon vieux: So you have lost your manuscript. I am desolé for you. For myself I am delighted, better not to have any written evidence of all those months of which I am not proud. So you say are feel like killing yourself with frustration—good idea. A way to be rid of you once and for all. Good thing to know you are far away from me, though I must say Greece sounds pretty tempting, rowing in the sun and all that. I saw Lily yesterday. I went over and fucked her. I fucked her again and again. I like it even better now than before.' I hated the cold, callous way he described joining up with Lily again. No friendship, no affection, or was he just playing it tough? I thought of my last conversation with her when we talked of him and the act of love in general. I wondered now exactly where and how he had fucked her. I longed to tell Rachel. I could see her clever little face with her soft brown eyes and her sharp tongue saying, 'I told you Edouard was a pederast'. I laughed out loud. I read on, 'I see you have not changed. You still ask me questions and meddle in my affairs. I wish you'd mind your own business and let me mind mine. Love, Edouard. P.S. I dare not go to the bar again—your postcard from Florence put me to shame!'

I answered immediately. 'I am glad you are back with Lily. If I had not meddled you would still be scraping a miserable existence in Paris. Furthermore, you would be blind, dragged about by a trained dog, or by me, which would be even worse. At least a dog can't talk. So shut up!' The next letter came a few days later. 'Mon vieux—no good news this time. Jean Claude had an accident with his car in Oxford Circus, Michel hates his job, and mine has folded up. Lucien wrote from Nice where he is selling oysters. Lily is in hospital with skin eruptions. Pas gai, tout ça. I've been offered a job up north but I can't leave Lily now. She's a good girl after all.' There was no love in that remark, it was kindly, no more. I was upset by the news and rang Lily at once. To my surprise she had already returned home. Poor devil, I thought. For her job and with her wonderful skin, that mass of flawless ivory, a skin disease was death. I followed it up with a letter to each of them.

I sent Edouard to a woman friend whose family owned gambling clubs in London. 'Can you help,' I wrote. She wrote back immediately, poetically.

'Your Edouard came this morning, beautiful and spoilt, a suede jacketed Venus rising from the debris of my ground floor which thirty booted workmen are re-building. He arrived with a bouquet of roses in his hands. I shall try to help him.' By the same post came a letter from Edouard himself. When I picked it up I was not to know that it contained what I had been waiting for all this long year. It was a line or two written in a moment of awareness, a moment of affection. I could not believe it.

'I was so touched by your immediate concern for Lily and for me. Suddenly I saw you in a different light and realised what you are to me and the great friendship that is between us. I have forgotten the horrors of the past year. I feel I have a friend in you, a person I can come to, talk to, lean on and ask help from. I will come and spend some days with you soon.' He signed it, 'Edouard, ton copain, non pas ton amant.'—Your friend, not your lover.

So it was over, it was finished. That's how it had ended. Alright for me, because now the friendship could continue forever. So I had not wasted a year, I had made a friend. Something remained; he would still be in my life. We might yet have the holiday in Greece and I might yet fix up his apartment for him, help him, advise him, leave him all I had. This fortune I was so worried about bequeathing, this fortune I had not yet inherited and maybe would never inherit. I immediately rang Murray. 'I'm so happy, it's alright, all is well at last.' I told him about Edouard's letter. Murray waited for me to finish.

'Has he a job?' asked Murray, quick as ever.

'No he hasn't, and she's sick.'

'Well, of course he means it, means it now. He might come, he might not. He does anything that goes through his head at the moment. He has nothing to do and most of the time nothing goes through his head anyway. He's a nice boy alright, but not alright for you.' I laughed. Murray was so funny and so right. I had only to ring him to get the truth in all its right proportions. Even his tone of voice made me see what mattered.

A few days later I had a telephone message from Edouard saying he would be coming over to Paris on Monday, in eight days. He said he was filming and he would be through by then. I waited all week but no news came. By Wednesday, two days after he was due, I became irritated and wrote him a letter. 'Dear Edouard, I was delighted at the idea of your visit. You said you would be here two days ago and I am still without news of you. Of course, I could have telephoned, so could you. However, one should never get angry till one knows the truth. I am more anxious than angry.' Edouard telephoned on receipt of my letter.

'I was doing that film I told you about, and I didn't know when it would finish.'

'Then ring me, tell me—if you can't do better than that, forget me and the whole thing.' I never thought the day would come when I would give him a chance to drop me.

'I'll come next Monday,' he said. 'I'm sorry I didn't let you know.' Then three days later a card came from Lily. 'What fun that we will all be together in Paris soon. Love, Lily.' I wrote instantly to Edouard and Lily. 'What fun and how marvellous for whom? I thought you were coming, Edouard, as a gesture of friendship to me. If you are passing through with Lily, I don't want it. Not this time.' Again he telephoned. He said it was a misunderstanding and he would be coming alone to see me. Then Lily rang some days later.

'I hope he doesn't come on the weekend—I am usually alone then and have little work. We are very happy and he is much changed. He is depressed now that he is without a real job. He thinks I don't want him to work so he will need me more.' She spoke for twenty minutes caring little about the cost.

On Friday evening I dined at Murray's. I had had Edouard on my mind since early morning. I was neither nostalgic, nor angry, nor excited. He was just there, in my head. I telephoned my hotel to see if there were any messages. I returned from Murray's at midnight to find one waiting for me in my room. 'Mlle Lily called from London. M. Edouard will be at Orly at midnight.' Edouard drove directly to my hotel in a taxi. In the meantime, I ran up to my room and washed myself and my hair. A shampoo makes me look younger and the hair a little thicker. I went down to meet the taxi. There was a strong wind and Edouard ran to the front door, his collar turned up and his hair flying over his face; he took great leaps as he ran from the taxi to the door. It might have been yesterday—I knew his every gesture, every turn of the body, every twist of the mouth.

'Come up and have a wash,' I said, 'And then we'll go out.'

'I'm tired,' he said. And he told me of his life in London. 'I lost my croupier job through gambling, it isn't allowed, so I did this film thing instead. It's unpaid, but I like it, I love films. I want to get into them.'

I could have hit him. 'Edouard, you stupid oaf, what do you think I was offering you last year?'

'I wasn't ready then,' he said. 'I am now.'

'But I have lost my contacts,' I said. He knew I had been friendly with Jane Opal, the most photographed film star of the moment. I had even been photographed in the papers with her and her new husband. 'I'll get in touch with them,' I said. 'Maybe they will help.'

The next day I let him sleep late. Silently I opened his door and stood looking at him. The maid who does my room came and said, 'How good looking the young man is.'

He was sleeping with his mouth open. I woke him by working a piece of tangerine into his mouth, just as I had done a year and a half before. I sat on his bed and rubbed his head. Then he got up and shaved. All his old habits were coming back to me. How he shaved standing up in his underpants, how after shaving he lifted a tin of talcum powder high above his face and tapped it out as it fell all over his face and the floor. We passed a happy quiet day together.

The next morning Jane telephoned. I told her Edouard was here.

'The one whose photos you showed me in Hollywood?'

'Yes,' I said.

'Bring him round to the studio,' she said. We went. Jane was filming so I didn't go up and talk to her. She noticed me at the end of a scene she was acting.

'Where's your friend?' she shouted.

'There,' I pointed. Edouard stood behind a big studio light.

'Turn the light on that man,' Jane ordered. 'Hello, glad to know you. I recognise you from your pictures,' she said, stopping the filming. Edouard was pleased.

I took him to a party that night but he was tired. There were pretty girls but he wasn't interested. He returned home with me and I sat on the floor by his hide. He drew me to him and pushed the hair away from my bald patch.

'You're losing your hair,' he said. 'I hope we will still be friends when you are quite bald. I hope one day to be rich and famous and that people will say, "What does that famous Edouard see in that bald man?" ' Before going to bed I made him put some 'Pour un Homme' under his arms. I wanted to see if he smelled the same as in the old days.

He was not in his room the next morning when I came in, though he usually slept late. Not long after he came to my room. 'I think I have done the right thing, so don't be cross,' he said, and he handed me the money I had given him the day before we left France together. 'You said you were short.'

Later that afternoon friends dropped in and I showed them Edouard's pictures, asking them which ones should be blown up for use in the future. I bent down to take out an envelope full, when I noticed it was dripping wet. I remembered a few days before having spilt a glass of water and wondering where the water had disappeared to. It had fallen into the attaché case containing Edouard's photos and all the letters from him and Lily. As I took the wet sticky mess, Edouard recognised his handwriting.

'Those are mine,' he said. 'Show me.' I handed him one and he started to read it. He looked suddenly sad and he handed it back to me.

'I don't want to read them, destroy them.' I looked at the last letter. It was the one he had written to Michel. 'The Queer fixed it all for me. Who wants his bloody money anyway.'

'You tear it up, Edouard.' Silently he tore them all up, Lily's and Edouard's letters. Then I picked up the envelope that was also soggy and coming to pieces. I was about to tear it up as well, when I saw a letter still stuck in it. I pulled it out. It was another of Edouard's. I read the beginning of it: 'Suddenly I saw you in a different light and I realised what you meant to me . . .'